"He's from here," Caroline said. "He grew up here. It's logical he'd come here. But it's also possible he came here looking for me."

"Why in the hell would you take a job in Denver if you knew he was from here?" Brooke asked, incredulous.

"Because I didn't think it mattered. I thought he was going to be in jail for thirty-five years. I wasn't going to let him being from Denver keep me from my best job offer."

"You seem pretty calm about the possibility he came here looking for you," Matty observed.

Caroline shrugged. "I'm past being afraid. I've been afraid for fifteen years. Now I'm mad."

"She's right, you know," Brooke said. "Let's take the offensive for once. Have some control over what happens to us."

Jane was confused. "I'm not sure what you're proposing here. Are you saying we should try to find him?"

Caroline and Brooke looked across the table at each other and nodded.

"And then what?" Jane asked logically. "What will you do then?"

"Kill him," Caroline said calmly. "Kill the son-of-a-bitch."

About the Author

Jeane Harris lives with her son and a cat who possesses a rear end the size of a Volkswagen.

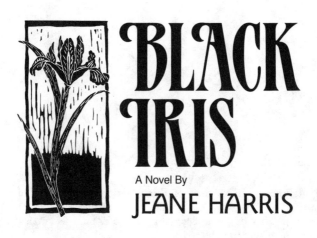

BLACK IRIS

A Novel By

JEANE HARRIS

The Naiad Press, Inc.
1991

Copyright © 1991 by Jeane Harris

Printed in the United States of America on acid-free paper
First Edition

Edited by Christine Cassidy
Cover design by Pat Tong and Bonnie Liss
    (Phoenix Graphics)
Typeset by Sandi Stancil

Library of Congress Cataloging-in-Publication Data

Harris, Jeane, 1948–
    Black iris / by Jeane Harris.
    p.   cm.
    ISBN 0-941483-68-1 : $8.95
    I. Title.
PS3558.A6463B55   1991
813'.54--dc20   90-6420
                                                            CIP

This book is for Carla.
Finally.

Acknowledgments

The author would like to thank the following people for their encouragement, love and support during the writing of this novel:

MSF, Robin, Jill, Annie, Hollace, Schof, Bunn E., Mike Devito, Joel, Sally W., Marica, Ellen, "Hammer" Adams, Eric, Tree, Stick, Scouffie, Team Beckelman, and finally, my little Bucko, who didn't believe in the book but always believed in me.

CHAPTER ONE

One of the virtues Caroline Jordan enjoyed most about her office at the university was the view of the mountains through the large window on the west wall. Over a ten-year period, the brown cloud of air pollution had gradually obscured her view, but it was still a breathtaking sight on those special days when the wind scrubbed the air clean and brought the front range of the Rocky Mountains into blue crystalline focus again. May held many of those kinds of days, and as she watched from her window, the sun began to disappear behind the mountain

1

tops, staining the clouds pink and orange in a last gaudy display.

Arching her back to ease the stiffness from sitting so long, she looked away from the mountain sunset to the stack of ungraded final papers and exams on her desk. She'd worked for three days straight and still wasn't caught up. Stifling a yawn, she thought once again how glad she would be when the term was ended and she was done for three months. Then, she thought, she'd be able to spend more evenings with Susan. She pushed her dark brown hair away from her eyes, ruefully remembering that she had forgotten to call her hairstylist again.

She walked down the hall to the staff room of the Education Department which was deserted, as it usually was on a Friday afternoon during final exam week, and took a can of Pepsi from a small refrigerator in the corner. She smiled slightly as she recalled Jane's standard lecture on caffeine addiction.

Back in her office, Caroline admitted that she had felt better since taking Jane's advice about her diet. But, she thought, Pepsi and cigarettes were two addictions she hadn't yet conquered. Thinking about her other addiction made Caroline think of Susan again, and she pushed the whole notion from her mind. She had too much work to do.

She looked around her office in dismay. Usually neat and uncluttered, it was a mess. Her two Boston ferns were dead or dying, books tumbled from the bookcases onto the floor which was littered with paper, notebooks and dead leaves from the ferns. Her normally spotless desk was buried under a mound of journals, folders and paper. She swiveled

2

her chair back to the window and winced as the old springs squealed in protest. Jane had bought the chair two years ago at a garage sale.

Jane spent many Saturdays prowling through flea markets and garage sales in search of bargains. Once Caroline had allowed herself to be talked into accompanying Jane on one of her expeditions.

"Why anyone would pay good money for this junk is simply beyond me," Caroline had said disparagingly. "It's probably infested with vermin."

"This is *not* junk," Jane huffed indignantly, as she wrestled an old dressmaker's dummy into the back of her Jeep. "It's an antique. It's art. A reminder of the past."

"I don't like to be reminded of the past," Caroline had replied.

"Well, I do," Jane said. "I love the past. You couldn't live without the past."

"Yes, I could," Caroline had asserted flatly, thinking at the time how much the conversation symbolized their differences. It was true, Caroline thought. They were total opposites. Jane was an artist — creative, impulsive, and theatrical. Her upstairs studio contained a potter's wheel, a loom, an enormous battered table covered with tubes of paint, palettes and knives, and three large easels, each holding a painting or drawing in varying stages of completion. Such disorder and chaotic creativity made Caroline nervous. She had realized early in their relationship that while she could never live with Jane, she could never live without her. So they had compromised. Jane lived in the upstairs part of their old Victorian mansion and Caroline lived on the main floor. They had separate entrances and, in many ways, separate lives. But, Caroline thought, they loved each other deeply and passionately. But differently.

The ringing phone on Caroline's desk jolted her out of her reverie. As she reached for it she noticed her hand was shaking.

"Listen," Matty said, "would you all like to have dinner with us this weekend at the Magnolia? We feel like we've been hibernating for months."

"That sounds great," Caroline said. "I guess Evie is doing better, huh?"

"Yeah, all things considered, she's doing fine. Her therapy is going well. She's sleeping better now. Things are progressing. Eleanor Hutchinson — do you know her? She owns that bookstore over by Jane's gallery — is taking her kid and some other kids to opening day at Elitch's. Then in the evening they're having some kind of concert."

Caroline smiled. "God, Eleanor always was a saint. Who's paying her to do this selfless act?"

"You know, I was in the bookstore the other day and she told me she actually *likes* taking the kids to rock concerts. But I think the real reason she's doing it is because her boy likes my daughter. Evie talks about Walker incessantly, and it seems like every time I come home, he's standing in front of my refrigerator looking for something to eat."

Caroline laughed. "Sounds serious to me."

"Well, I'm glad she hasn't let this whole thing — I don't know, keep her from . . . you know . . ."

"Liking boys?"

"Oh, Carrie," Matty sighed. "I don't know what I thought. That she would be forever changed. That she'd hate boys or me or all of us. I suppose she is

4

forever changed. She wouldn't let any of her friends come and see her when she was still in the hospital. She banished Walker for almost a month, but he was pretty good about it. He's very sensitive and sweet. And Evie *was* fearful and kind of withdrawn for a while. Her therapy with Sandy has really helped. Actually we've all been going — it's helped all of us. Her casts are off, her jaw isn't wired anymore. The swelling has almost completely gone down. It doesn't look like there's going to be any permanent physical damage."

"Any leads on the guy who did it?"

"No," Matty admitted. "And Brooke is so angry about it. She just can't understand why they haven't found him."

"I have a hard time with that too," Caroline said, her voice hard-edged. "The sooner they find the bastard the better."

"My sentiments exactly." Matty paused. "Well, anyway, we decided we need a night out together."

"Have you talked to Jane yet?" Caroline asked.

"No, I tried calling you at home but no one answered. I guess Jane's at the gallery."

"That's probably it," Caroline said. "She goes there almost every night. I really haven't seen her lately, except in the morning sometimes. She's usually gone running when I first get up. I'm usually rushing around getting ready for work and when I get home in the evening, she's either gone to bed or she's at the gallery."

"Spending a lot of time with Susan after work?" Matty asked pointedly.

"Susan who?"

"Oh, I heard a rumor you were seeing someone."

"Who told you that?" Caroline demanded.

"Three guesses, Carrie."

"So Jane told Brooke already, huh?"

"Seems so. Maybe Jane's avoiding you for a reason," Matty theorized. "You know how she is. She'll avoid this for as long as she can."

"Well, why shouldn't she? It doesn't mean anything."

"You sure? You sound pretty distracted."

"I think so." Caroline paused, pushing her hair back from her face. "I don't know, Matt. I can't seem to get anything done. I'm missing appointments, I'm late for everything. I'm a mess."

"Is it serious with Susan? Is it love?" Matty asked.

"Are you kidding? She's twenty-three years old. Anyway, Jane understands. She knows how I am. She knows I love her."

"Whatever you say. If you see Jane, ask her about Saturday, okay? Don't forget."

"Well, I'm sure Brooke will see her before I do, but okay," Caroline promised.

For the first time since the attack on Matty's thirteen-year-old daughter, Caroline felt optimistic about Matty and Brooke's relationship. She had feared that the attack might force them apart and, at first, it seemed as though it would. Evie had been pulled from her bicycle at the zoo, dragged into bushes. She had not, thankfully, been raped — her attacker had been frightened off by someone approaching the scene — but she had been badly beaten, and Matty and Brooke had taken blame on themselves for allowing her to be at the zoo. But they seemed to be weathering the crisis. Caroline was glad. Over the years, she had become good friends with Jane's former college roommates.

She thought back to Matty's warning about Jane. Was she in danger of losing her? She dismissed the notion. Freedom was part of their bargain, like separate residences. Together, but separate. Besides, she'd had affairs before and, while Jane didn't like it, she had adjusted. Anyway, Caroline told herself, it wasn't her dating Susan McKay that was distressing Jane. It was the opening of Jane's gallery in August. And it wasn't her affair with Susan McKay that was causing Caroline's sleepless nights and making her forget her appointments. It was something else, Caroline fretted, something that she couldn't put her finger on.

Ever since she had seen Evie lying in the hospital bed, her arms in a cast, her lips split open, her face battered and swollen, she had not been able to put the image from her mind. It reminded her of so many things . . . things she had not thought of in a long time and had tried so hard to forget. Again, the phone rang beside her and this time she jumped.

She heard Susan's warm voice. "I had a collective meeting last night. Sorry I missed you."

"So what are Denver's most politically correct lesbians up to these days?"

"Oh, this and that," Susan said hurriedly. "Listen, I was wondering if you'd have dinner with me tonight at the Magnolia? I thought afterwards, maybe you would come up here to my house. I've been wanting you to see it. How about it?"

Caroline thought quickly. She wanted to say yes but Matty's words about Jane nagged in the back of her mind. Then the image of Evie in the hospital bed flashed through her mind.

"Sure. How about half an hour?"

The Steel Magnolia catered to all kinds of lesbians, although over the years Caroline had noticed that certain nights attracted certain kinds of women. On the weekdays, a more sedate, older crowd occupied the tables and booths, talking quietly, drinking coffee from the giant stainless-steel urn that the owners, Sandra Luther and Margaret Bailey, kept behind the bar. And most of the women who came in during the week came to eat dinner. Margaret's repertoire of recipes was short and simple — chili, spaghetti, burritos, meatloaf and steak — but the food was delicious and, compared to other restaurants in the area around the Denver Coliseum, relatively inexpensive. Steak night was a favorite. On Thursday nights during the summer and early fall, Margaret, in a large white apron and chef's hat, fired up the two large charcoal grills in the parking lot behind the bar and cooked steaks to order.

On the weekends, a younger group of women, some of them with wild, multi-hued hairstyles, and dressed in denim, leather, and even silk, crowded the dance floor, bouncing and jostling each other enthusiastically. Often, women in softball, rugby or soccer uniforms celebrated their victories or mourned their losses around the bar. It was a warm, companionable atmosphere, and it was rare that an argument or fight broke out that Margaret or Sandra couldn't handle themselves.

The building itself was a former warehouse converted into a bar. Divided into two major sections, it housed a good-sized dance floor and three regulation-sized pool tables. In front was the long oak bar that Margaret and Sandra had purchased at the auction of an old bar in Evergreen, along with the three pool tables, an old Wurlitzer jukebox and the tables and chairs that lined the partition separating the pool tables from the dance floor. Directly to the left of the bar was the small but well-equipped kitchen and pantry.

In the rear, the dance floor was surrounded by booths and tables. A short hallway led to two restrooms labeled "Dykes" and "More Dykes." Hanging plants, tended and watered by Margaret in a futile effort to keep them healthy, struggled to survive in the usually dark, smoky air. The walls were covered with pictures, all drawn or painted by lesbian artists, and, Caroline thought proudly as she entered the bar, some of them were Jane's. Those that weren't had been painted or drawn by women artists in the Women's Art Guild, an organization Jane had founded seven years ago to encourage Denver's women artists, many of them lesbians, to show their work.

Due to the early hour, only a few women were in the Steel Magnolia. Margaret walked around lighting candles on the tables and booths. Because it was a Friday night, soon a storm of women would arrive demanding drinks and food.

"Just got off work," Caroline told her. "I'm meeting Susan McKay for dinner."

"Ah-ha," Margaret said. "I've seen you two in here a lot lately."

"Don't you start on me, too," Caroline warned grumpily. "I've already had my lecture of the day from Matty."

"I never said a word." Margaret smiled. "How's Matty's little girl?"

"A lot better. She's out of the hospital. She's doing some therapy with Sandy Fuller, you know her? She's really good. So, I guess it's okay, everything considered."

"That's such a terrible thing. I feel so sorry for Matty and Brooke. Did they catch the bastard who did it yet?"

Caroline became aware that the jukebox was turned up so loud she could hardly hear. "No, not yet."

"They ought to have a trial right here when they do catch him," Margaret said.

Caroline felt the beginnings of a headache. "Could you turn down the music a little, babe?" she asked. "It's really loud." Margaret reached down and flicked the switch behind the bar. Caroline's temples were throbbing. "Fine. Better."

"Well, like I said. They ought to let us have a trial right here in the bar. Twelve women, good and true. We'd give him justice."

Caroline lit a cigarette and glanced toward the door in time to see Susan McKay come in. Her light brown hair was plaited into a single braid down her back, and she wore a pair of brightly colored Hawaiian shorts and a red cotton T-shirt. Her ruddy cheeks and fresh face cheered Caroline immediately, and she smiled in appreciation as she hugged Susan. Her headache was suddenly forgotten.

"Hi," Susan whispered into Caroline's ear, sending

10

a wave of electricity down her spine. "I love your outfit. It's so — femme."

"I didn't have time to go home and change," Caroline lied. She blushed, knowing Susan saw through the lie. She wondered why Susan always had this effect on her.

Susan was only twenty-three years old and to Caroline, at nearly thirty-eight, she seemed ridiculously young. Indeed, Caroline had often told herself, Susan was younger than many of her students. Susan was a woman of endless energy, fiery feminist politics and tireless good humor. Her enthusiastic, sometimes boisterous manner put some people off, Caroline knew. Margaret once said that Susan had all the finesse of a steamroller, but Caroline found her irrepressible nature endearing and refreshing. Being around her always made Caroline feel younger. Besides, Caroline admitted, Susan was extremely attractive, her impressive physique the result of a strenuous weight lifting regimen, and she had an incredible physical presence that was blatantly sexual. As Susan ordered a beer, Caroline marveled at the humor in her lively blue eyes, how they seemed to take in everything around her and smile approval on everyone.

Caroline got up from her bar stool and chose a table near the back of the bar where she could see the entrance. Sitting opposite Susan, she looked over the menu, then leaned back in her chair and remembered the first time she and Jane and Brooke and Matty had come to the Magnolia during Jane's first visit to Denver. It had been a long time ago, Caroline thought.

Susan was looking directly at Caroline's breasts,

11

and Caroline felt her face redden. Caroline had a sudden image of Susan's mouth on her breast and her face grew warmer still. She was glad Susan couldn't see her blush in the dimly lit room.

"Have you been thinking about what you want?" Susan asked, tracing a line down Caroline's forearm with her finger.

"Actually, I was just thinking about the first time Matty and Brooke and Jane and I came in here. It was when the bar first opened. Do you know that story about how Brooke and Matty lived together for almost three years before Brooke told her she was a lesbian and that she was in love with her?"

"No," Susan said. "That's impossible. Nobody could do that. Especially Brooke."

"Well, it's true," Caroline insisted. "Believe me, I know. I was there. They had been roommates in college — Jane, Matty and Brooke — and Brooke never told either of them she was gay."

"That was really awful about their kid," Susan said. She looked around for Margaret and motioned her over to their table. They ordered salads, chili and another round of drinks.

After Margaret left, Susan leaned forward and Caroline looked at her breasts pressing against the edge of the table. Two weeks earlier Susan had first kissed her in the parking lot outside the bar. They were standing by Caroline's car saying goodnight when Susan suddenly took Caroline in her arms and pressed her against the car. Holding Caroline's head, Susan had kissed her deeply. Then, running her hands up Caroline's arms, she had caressed the sides of her breasts gently, teasingly. Caroline had been left breathless from the kiss and almost allowed herself to be talked into going home with Susan to spend the night. But in spite of what everyone else thought, she had not yet been to bed with Susan, and that probably made the flirting even more delicious. Anticipation was half the fun, Caroline thought, looking at Susan's full, sensuous lips and imagining them on her own. She knew Susan would be as wild and uninhibited in her lovemaking as she was about everything else — especially eating. Caroline smiled to herself; Susan had a healthy appetite.

"Speaking of Matty and Brooke, how's their kid? What's her name? How old is she?"

"Evie," Caroline told her, pulling her hand away. She felt her headache coming back. "She's almost thirteen. She's doing a lot better. It was awful though. Matty and Brooke have been blaming themselves a lot."

"I can imagine," Susan murmured sympathetically. "The collective has a fund for victims, you know. Mostly rape, but it's also for muggings and abuse victims. For counseling, whatever."

"That's a good idea," Caroline said. "I know Matty got Evie into counseling right after it happened. Matty has good insurance too. They're taking her to Disneyworld this summer."

"She'll love that. I went there when I was in college. I went to college in Florida, you know. Florida State. It was great fun." She looked at

Caroline intently. "You know, Doc, you look tired."
She grinned. "Nothing a quiet night in the
mountains wouldn't cure. Or a not-so-quiet night."

Caroline returned her grin. "I am pretty tired
these days. Been working late at school."

"Well, I think you're ready for a night off, don't
you?"

Caroline leaned forward and brushed her lips
softly against Susan's. Susan responded by pulling
her closer and deepening their kiss. Caroline's pulse
quickened as Susan's tongue probed more insistently.

"Hey! Do you guys want to neck or eat?"

Caroline pulled away, embarrassed, and looked up
as Margaret put their food on the table.

"Be careful," Margaret warned Susan. "The chili's
hot."

After she left, Susan looked at Caroline
appreciatively. "Not as hot as you. God, what a
kiss."

Caroline watched as Susan attacked her bowl of
chili. She herself ate her salad slowly and without
appetite, the headache nagging at the back of her
skull.

"So . . . tell me more of this story about Matty
and Brooke."

"Well, it was when I first came to Denver, right
after I got my Ph.D. I had a job here and Jane
stayed in San Diego for the first year. Then she
came out to visit me and since Matty and Brooke
still lived in Boulder, I invited them down to my
apartment for dinner."

"And they'd been living together for how long?"

"Oh, about three years. Matty's husband got
killed in Vietnam. Anyway, Brooke just never got up

14

enough nerve to tell Matty she was gay, and then when she fell in love with her, well, it was funny. She kept writing Jane all these letters saying she was going to tell Matty. And Jane'd always ask 'When?' and Brooke would always say, 'Soon.' It got to be a big joke between us."

"I don't understand why Brooke didn't just tell her."

"Well, at first I think Brooke didn't want to scare Matty away. Matty'd been through a lot — her husband got killed, she had a baby, she was working on a Ph.D. too — all that stuff was a lot to handle. Brooke didn't think Matty was ready to hear her best friend say, 'Oh, by the way, I'm in love with you.'"

"I can understand that at *first*," Susan admitted. "But *three years?*"

"I don't understand how she did it either," Caroline said. "But she did." She pushed her salad bowl away. "Anyway, Jane came to visit me and we had them over for dinner. And we were sitting around after dinner, drinking some wine. Actually, Matty and I were drinking wine and Jane and Brooke were in the kitchen doing the dishes, smoking dope and getting stoned out of their minds, giggling and carrying on like they always do. And after they came out into the living room, Matty started telling this story about a woman in their dorm who Matty described as, get this, 'inappropriately fond of other women.'"

"Oh, God," Susan's eyes grew wide. "What did you guys say?"

"Well, everybody got *real* quiet. I was speechless. Brooke and Jane looked at the floor. I mean, the silence was definitely awkward. And Matty was puzzled — naturally. She didn't know what she'd said to make everybody so embarrassed. So she looked around and asked, 'Did I say something wrong?' And nobody said anything. So she said, 'I guess I did.' And Jane was a big help. She just started tying and untying her shoe. And I kept waiting for one of them to say something because I sure wasn't going to."

Susan had forgotten her food. "What happened then?"

"Well, finally Matty, bright woman that she is, got it. She looked at all of us, probably thought about Brooke and all their history — she finally said, 'Oh, no. I — are you all?' And Jane and Brooke nodded. I stood up and said, 'I have to walk the dog now. I hear him whining at the back door.' "

Susan laughed. "Great. I love it. Terrific trick — getting him to whine on cue like that."

Caroline looked down at her salad bowl. "Well, that's the funny part."

"What? Your dog whining?"

"No," Caroline admitted sheepishly. "I didn't have a dog."

Susan stared at her for a moment and then let out a great whoop of laughter. She continued to laugh until, out of curiosity, Sandy and Margaret came over to their table.

"What's so funny?" Sandy asked, smiling herself.

"Great!" Susan pounded the table with her hand. "That's great: 'I didn't have a dog.' " She laughed again.

Sandra and Margaret smiled at each other and

then at Caroline. "Oh, you're telling her the Matty and Brooke story."

Susan looked at Caroline. "What? Does everybody know this story but me?"

Sandra patted Susan's head. "It happened when you were just a baby." She looked at Margaret. "How old would Susan have been then? Ten? Eleven?"

"Oh, surely not that old," Margaret joked, as they walked back to the bar. "Maybe seven or eight."

"Hey, I'm twenty-three years old," Susan yelled at them. "That's old enough." She looked back at Caroline, smiling. "Am I old enough?"

Caroline looked into Susan's eyes, alight with good humor, and winked at her. "Oh, yes. I think you're definitely old enough." She laced her fingers firmly with Susan's.

Susan grinned lazily and pushed her empty chili bowl away. "Are you ready to get out of here and go someplace where we can be alone?"

Caroline's breath caught in her throat and suddenly she realized that she wanted to be alone with Susan more than anything — somewhere where Susan could undress her slowly and fan the flame of passion that was making her feverish.

"Yes," Caroline murmured, looking deep into Susan's eyes. "I'm ready."

"Okay, once we're in the canyon, the road curves a lot and it's hard to see. So follow me close."

Caroline leaned across the booth and kissed Susan gently on the mouth. "As close as I can."

CHAPTER TWO

He was walking alone down Nineteenth Street and Vine with his Louisville Slugger. The bat felt good in his hand. The weight and balance made him feel powerful. A sign on a light pole in front of him said: QUIET HOSPITAL ZONE. He stopped in front of the hospital. There were lights along the driveway and cars parked along the street. Across the street from the entrance was an underground parking lot. It was dark there. He crossed the street and walked down the ramp into the parking lot.

Standing in the shadows behind a round pillar,

he watched two nurses in green scrub suits walking down the steps of the hospital. He smiled. He would take whichever one came his way. He watched as they waved to each other and walked away in different directions. One of them started walking toward the parking lot.

He reached down and touched the front of his pants.

Hard. He knew he would be.

He leaned the baseball bat against a parked car behind him so he would have both hands free when he had to grab her. He watched her coming down the ramp toward him. She walked with her head down. Maybe she was tired. That was good. She wouldn't fight as much. When she was almost even with his hiding place behind the pillar, he stepped out from the shadows and smiled at her. She looked startled and quickened her pace. He reached behind him, picked up the baseball bat and hurried to catch up with her.

Suddenly, she whirled around to face him. Her expression was hard and indignant. "What do you want, buddy?"

His hand touched the front of his pants again. Stupid bitch. She knew what he wanted. They all tried to pretend that they didn't know. Just like the Jordan woman. Just like the young girl.

But they did know.

CHAPTER THREE

Caroline looked up at the loft that extended over the living room of Susan's house. "This is an incredible house," she called to Susan, who was in the kitchen opening a bottle of wine.

"Thanks. I've spent a lot of time and money fixing it up. What do you think of the loft?"

Caroline looked at the ladder apprehensively. "I like the idea, but I'm not sure about the ladder — especially in a skirt."

Susan walked into the room carrying two glasses of wine and handed one to Caroline. Her arm encircled Caroline's waist. "I'd like to take off your skirt and see what's underneath." Susan pressed Caroline's pelvis against her own. "Do you have a slip on underneath your skirt?" she murmured.

Caroline's mind went blank. She was distracted by Susan's warm hand caressing the curve of her back. "I think so."

Susan released her and moved away, smiling. She pulled Caroline to her and unfastened her skirt, which fell to the floor. "Well, now. What a pretty slip." She put her hands on Caroline's shoulders and turned her around so she was facing the ladder. "So — go ahead."

Caroline leaned back against Susan and nuzzled against her neck. "How do I know you won't look up my slip while I'm climbing?"

Susan's breath was warm on her shoulders as she kissed Caroline's neck. "I won't look. Trust me."

When she reached the top rung of the ladder, Caroline turned around and took the glasses from Susan, who followed her into the room. Suddenly they were in each other's arms, kissing passionately. Caroline savored Susan's strong arms around her, Susan's hands gently kneading and stroking her through the thin slip. Eventually, she broke their kiss and caught Caroline's bottom lip between her teeth.

"I love the way you kiss me," Susan said against her mouth. She unbuttoned Caroline's blouse. "And I love this slip." Susan moved her mouth down to Caroline's breasts and lavished kisses above the lacy fringe. Excitement raced like white heat through Caroline's veins, and she felt herself growing wet with desire. Groaning with need and pleasure, she

21

ground her hips against Susan and pushed her tongue deep into Susan's mouth. Susan responded eagerly, stroking Caroline's tongue with her own and soon her murmurs of pleasure mingled with Caroline's. Susan's tongue licked her lips and flicked at the corner of her mouth. She felt Susan's hands stroking her shoulders, and her slip fell in a silken puddle at her feet.

"You are so sweet," Susan breathed into her ear, her warm breath tickling deliciously. Reaching behind her, Susan unhooked Caroline's bra which soon joined her slip and blouse on the floor. "You're so beautiful," Susan sighed. Susan stood back to admire the rich fullness of Caroline's breasts, but soon her hands were stroking the dark nipples which sprang to life under her hands. Susan slid Caroline's underpants down over her hips and finally, Caroline stood before her naked. Susan drew Caroline back into her arms and let her fingers explore the sweet slickness between her legs, parting the soft, wet folds of flesh and stroking around the hard bud of her clitoris.

"God, yes." Caroline spread her legs to allow Susan's fingers to glide inside her, but she felt her knees buckle and grabbed Susan's shoulders. "I'm going to faint if we don't lie down."

Susan smiled at her. She bent down and put her arm behind Caroline's legs, lifting her effortlessly in her arms. Moved by the tenderness of the gesture, Caroline buried her face in Susan's neck.

Susan lowered her to the bed, and Caroline could see her smiling at her in the dark. Then Susan traced a wet path with her tongue up the inside of Caroline's thigh.

Suddenly her mouth was where her hand had been before and Caroline's mind reeled with pleasure. There was only Susan's mouth parting her and her tongue thrusting deeply inside her, sucking and stroking. And then, Caroline found, she couldn't think anymore.

When Caroline was able to focus her vision again, she was aware that she was looking up at the night sky. She blinked once and saw the stars and a sliver of moon glimmering. She pulled Susan up to her and kissed her, tasting herself on her lips. "Wonderful," she murmured.

"What?" Susan asked, mischievously. "Me — or the view?"

"Hmmmm." Caroline enjoyed the warmth of Susan's body, now naked like her own, pressing against the warm, full length of her. "Both. You and the view. Both gorgeous." She stroked Susan's leg and pressed her knee firmly between Susan's legs. Susan murmured her pleasure and leaned into Caroline's knee.

"Like my skylight?" she asked, sifting Caroline's silky hair through her fingers. "I put it in myself."

"Did you now?" Caroline asked. "My, my. You are a multi-talented woman." She cupped Susan's small, perfect breasts in her hands and gently stroked the pink nipples until they grew hard. "Do you like this?"

"Yes. It feels so good." Susan gasped when Caroline twisted her nipple gently between her fingers. "Do it again."

"Anything," Caroline promised, doing it again. "Anything for you now."

"Just make love to me," Susan pleaded. "That's all."

Caroline smiled in the dark and kissed her stomach. "It's a deal," she whispered and willingly bent to her work.

"Are you all right? What are you doing over there?" Susan sat up in bed and pushed her hair out of her eyes.

Caroline turned away from the window. "Nothing, babe. You drifted off to sleep and I just decided to get up and look at the moonlight." She sighed and looked back at the view. "It's so peaceful up here — so beautiful. It must be wonderful to live up here all the time."

Susan got out of bed and padded over to the window. She put her arms around Caroline and held her close. "You're freezing. Come back to bed and get warm."

Caroline allowed Susan to lead her back to the bed. Susan looked at Caroline. "What's the matter? Why can't you sleep?"

"I don't know," Caroline admitted. "It's really weird. I've been so out of it lately. It's like . . . nothing is clear or focused."

"Maybe you're in love," Susan teased her gently.

Caroline took her face in her hands and grew serious. "You're right. I *am* in love. With Jane. I have been in love with her for almost thirteen years. You need to understand that."

Susan turned her head and kissed Caroline's palm. "I understand. I just don't understand . . ." She gestured helplessly. "This."

Caroline looked away. "Jane and I have an understanding. I'm not very good at monogamy. I couldn't have been with Jane this long if I had to be monogamous. So — we compromise. I have other lovers and we stay together."

"Does she have other lovers too?" Susan wanted to know.

"Not that I'm aware of. I just want you to understand that I'm not trying to get out of my relationship with Jane by going to bed with you."

Susan shook her head. "Okay, I understand." She pushed a strand of hair away from Caroline's face. "Why don't you stay here with me tonight?"

Caroline shook her head. "No, I've got to go home."

"Okay. No problem."

Caroline sighed and settled back into the pillows. "I've had insomnia so bad. I get up every two hours and pace around. I can't eat. I feel nauseated all the time."

"Maybe you're pregnant," Susan joked.

"I don't know what's wrong. I feel stressed out."

"How long have you felt this way?" Susan asked. "Maybe you should go to the doctor."

"I don't know. I suppose I've been worried about Matty and Brooke and upset about Evie." She stopped.

"I can understand that. After all, they're good friends. You've known them a long time. All this must be really hard on them."

"Brooke's mad. She has a short fuse anyway and

25

this has really sent her into orbit. Plus, she blames herself for not watching Evie closer. Jane says Brooke wants to find the guy and kill him."

Susan nodded. "Yeah, I've seen Brooke lose it a couple of times. I used to play softball with her on a team out in Aurora. We were playing some straight team one night and they had this asshole coach who was really abusive to his players. We were all mad at him, but Brooke was really getting steamed. Finally, he called a woman on his team a stupid cunt when she struck out. Brooke was behind the plate catching when it happened. You should have seen her — she threw her mask at him and then went after him with an aluminum bat." Susan chuckled. "It was great. She chased him into the parking lot and whacked the side of his car."

Caroline smiled and shook her head. "That sounds exactly like her."

"Well, if more women would get mad once in a while and get even, we'd probably be better off." Susan reached over to the nightstand and handed Caroline her glass.

Caroline sipped the wine. She felt her headache coming back. "Yeah, maybe so."

"Maybe nothing," Susan countered. "Listen, if more women got revenge on men who fucked with them, there'd be fewer rapes."

"Revenge?" Caroline felt the muscles in her neck tense. Her temples throbbed with pain.

"Yeah, revenge. You know, getting even. An eye for an eye."

"I thought that's what the police were for."

"Bullshit!" Susan sneered. "How much good have the police done for Evie?" She sat up in bed. "Listen, let me tell you a story about something that happened to me while I was in college in Massachusetts."

Caroline's head pulsated with pain and she closed her eyes. "Do you have any aspirin handy?"

"Sure. Right here." She smiled. "Handy for hangovers." She shook out two aspirins and Caroline washed them down with her wine. "Better?"

Caroline nodded. "Go ahead." The wine tasted sour and she set the glass on the nightstand.

"Okay, I belonged to this Rape Task Force. We were just playing around at first. You know, making up posters and giving lectures in the girls' dorms on how to carry a bottle opener on your key ring, avoid dark corners of the campus, always know who you're going out with — you know, mostly self-defense, common sense kind of stuff. But then . . ." Susan paused dramatically. "Something happened. We got serious." She looked at Caroline. "Hey, are you okay? You look like you're really in pain."

"My head hurts," Caroline said. "I think maybe it's a migraine or something."

"Here. Turn over and I'll rub your neck. Most headaches start in the neck muscles. You can usually get rid of them by just massaging these two spots in the neck." She pushed her fingers into the base of Caroline's neck and began to gently rub them. Caroline felt some of the tension recede, but her temples still throbbed.

"So what happened?" Caroline asked. "What did you do?"

"Well, it started when a friend of mine in the dorm was raped. She was working as a barmaid in a hangout for the college crowd. Lots of kids from

Florida State hung out there. Anyway, one of the guys who worked in the kitchen offered to take her home one night when it was raining."

Caroline rolled over and sat up. "Thanks. It's much better now. Go on."

"Well, my friend said normally she would have refused, but her car was in the shop and it was raining. You know, the guy worked with her. She thought it would be okay. But it wasn't. He drove her to some neighborhood she didn't know and raped her."

Caroline began to tremble.

"Are you okay?" Susan asked. "Is your headache back?"

"No, I'm okay," Caroline assured her. "Go ahead."

"She tried to get away but he was just flat out stronger than she was and all she got for resisting was a couple of black eyes and a split lip. Then he took her home. Can you believe it?" Susan grimaced. "The arrogant asshole."

"Did she go to the police?" Caroline asked.

"No," Susan said. "She didn't. She came to me. She knew I was on the Rape Task Force and she wanted to know what she should do. I told her I thought going to the cops was bullshit. Nothing they do to rapists is bad enough. Send 'em to jail for six months or something. I took her to a meeting of the task force and we all talked about it." Susan smiled sheepishly. "I made a kind of impassioned speech for revenge. And when it was all over, we decided to get even."

"Even? What do you mean?"

"I mean, we decided to kidnap the asshole and rape him."

28

"How did you do it?" Caroline knew her voice sounded hollow.

"Well, it was pretty easy really. We sent one of the women into the restaurant a couple of days later with a message for the guy that he had an emergency phone call from his family at home and when he ran outside to his car a bunch of us jumped out of a van and tossed him in. There were three of us, and *we* were just flat out stronger." She grinned. "We tied him up with clothesline. This one woman, Cathy Baxter, was a cowgirl from Wyoming. She hog-tied the bastard. She rode him like a bull while we tied him up." Susan laughed. "It was great. We took him to Gloria Delgado's father's beach house —"

"Weren't you afraid he'd recognize some of you?"

"Naw. We didn't care anyway. We figured he'd be too embarrassed to say a bunch of women kidnapped and raped him. We did freak out every time we saw a cop car though. We were scared. But we were also mad. We were feeding on each other's energy and anger. Nobody talked about backing out or letting him go. We all stayed pretty cool."

She paused to take a sip of wine. "So, we had a little trial. Holly, the woman he raped, told everybody what had happened, identified him and we voted and found him guilty. Very simple. His mother wasn't there to tell us what a good little boy he'd been, no girlfriend to wring her hands saying he'd been with her that night. None of that bullshit. He was pretty cocky at first. After the initial shock wore off, he kept saying he'd get loose and rape all of us and our sisters and our mothers too. But when he realized that we actually had him and weren't going

29

to let him go, he was scared. He started to seriously piss his pants."

"What did you do to him?" Caroline asked, her voice shaking.

"We decided on . . ." She paused and looked at Caroline. "Do you want the gory details?"

Caroline shut her eyes. "No, I get the picture."

"Well," Susan concluded. "I'll tell you this. He *really* didn't like it."

"Did he ever tell anyone what happened?" Caroline asked softly.

"I doubt it." Susan laughed. "I can't imagine who he'd want to tell. Tell someone that a bunch of girls were able to toss him in a car and bugger him? And listen, no matter what anybody says, revenge is sweet. He did something despicable to a woman I cared about and I helped to punish him. He deserved it and I've never regretted it."

"You never felt guilty or anything?"

"No. Never," Susan said firmly. "We're conditioned to feel guilty about personal revenge so the courts can go on setting men who rape women and children free. Courts are mostly all run by men. Like everything else. Listen, I could almost guarantee that the guy who raped Holly never did it again."

Caroline got out of bed and began to dress.

"Are you sure you don't want to stay all night?" Susan asked. "It's nice up here in the morning." She grinned. "I make a great omelette."

"I'm sure you do," Caroline said, buttoning her blouse. "But I really need to get home and get some sleep. My head really hurts and I have to . . ." She trailed off uncertainly. "I just have to get home."

She leaned over and kissed Susan warmly. "Thank you for a wonderful evening. Really. I enjoyed it a lot. You're a wonderful lover. I really have to go now."

Susan held Caroline's lips against hers for a moment. "I'm crazy about you."

Caroline returned her kiss and gave Susan a quick squeeze. "You're just plain crazy." She turned around and descended the ladder. She slipped into her skirt and coat and went out into the night.

CHAPTER FOUR

Caroline tried to keep her mind calm as she drove down the curving road through Boulder Canyon. Although it was not especially cold, she found herself shivering and turned on the car heater. Her headache was worse, and she felt weak and exhausted. In Boulder she stopped at a 7-Eleven store, purchased a cup of coffee and Extra-Strength Tylenol, then started down the turnpike to Denver. She wondered if Jane had come home from the gallery yet and if she had noticed her absence.

Caroline smiled grimly. Of course she had

noticed. Caroline rarely felt guilty about any of her affairs but for some reason she felt uneasy about Susan. Her story of rape and revenge had been gruesome, but Susan hadn't expressed any regret over what she and her friends had done.

On one level, Caroline thought dispassionately, she felt great empathy for Susan and her friend. The man had done something horrible, and he deserved to be punished. In a way, she even relished the idea of his punishment. But another part of her recoiled from the idea of revenge. It was wrong, or so everyone said. Better to let the police handle it. It was too dangerous. Too . . . something. Caroline's headache distracted her. She couldn't think straight. Susan's story wouldn't go away. Revenge was Old Testament — primitive. An eye for an eye, tooth for a tooth.

She crumpled the coffee cup and threw it onto the floor of her car. She noted with disgust the abundance of paper, cans, sacks and cigarette wrappers on the floor. The back seat was stacked with books that needed to go back to the university library. She had never treated her car like this before. When had she stopped cleaning it, Caroline wondered. She pushed her hair out of her eyes. When had she stopped feeling hungry or attending to anything that mattered to her? Especially Jane, Caroline chided herself. She had a fleeting image of Susan's face, transformed by orgasm, and pushed it aside.

All she really needed, she told herself, was a good solid night's sleep. She hoped that Jane would be home when she arrived and that they could talk. As exciting as her encounters with Susan had been, she sharply missed the companionship and trust of her long relationship with her lover. Maybe Jane would sleep with her and hold her close. Then maybe the nightmares would be held at bay.

She drove slowly down Colfax Avenue. It was late, at least two in the morning, and though the coffee had helped keep her awake on the highway, she now felt the effects of the wine, the lovemaking and the sleepless nights. Suddenly a police car and ambulance came screaming up behind her. The sudden sound of the siren sent a surge of adrenalin through her and her heart pounded as she turned left onto Vine. She calmed herself; it was not unusual to see police cars and ambulances this time of night in Capitol Hill. Most of Denver's hospitals were only a few blocks north of Colfax.

She had only driven a block when suddenly her headlights illuminated a man running across the street directly in the path of her car. She slammed on the brakes and for an instant, before the man could reach the other side of the street, Caroline looked him full in the face. His hair was wildly disheveled. In his left hand, he carried a baseball bat, and when he saw the car bearing down on him, he raised it over his head, as if to ward off the car. Or to break through the windshield.

Caroline screamed and slammed her car into gear as she accelerated blindly.

Her tired body flooded with adrenalin, she turned the corner and sped up Eighteenth Street toward home. To Jane. To safety. She was shaking and sobbing when she pulled into the driveway and turned off the ignition. She gripped the steering wheel and with the determination of years of practice, she pushed the image of the man away, refusing to acknowledge it.

"I am Caroline Jordan," she whispered. "I'm thirty-eight years old — I have a Ph.D. — I'm an associate professor — I have a lover . . ." She continued her litany of comforting facts as she picked up her briefcase. What she had seen was impossible. She knew it. But she *had* seen it. The man in her nightmares.

With a supreme effort she pushed the image down and away from her. He was gone. She had not seen him. *Had not.* She looked up at the house, saw that Jane had left the porch light on and felt a rush of warmth and need for her. Once she was inside, with Jane's arms around her, everything would be normal. She opened the car door and hurried to the door, fumbling at the lock with trembling hands. She opened the door and, as she dropped her briefcase on the floor, felt her legs begin to buckle. She closed her eyes and took deep breaths, but she still sank to the floor, on her knees. Burying her face in her hands, she began to cry.

"No, no. It can't be. It's not him." Still crying, she reached for the edge of the sink to pull herself upright. She opened the cupboard and took down a glass. As she turned on the faucet, she looked down in the sink.

What she saw in the sink made her crush the glass in her hand.

A knife was lying in the sink.

Black-handled. Something on the blade that looked like — rust or . . . blood.

The shards of glass cut into her hand. Caroline could feel them under her feet too. As she walked along the highway. Cutting into the soles of her bare feet. As she cradled her broken arms against her body. Suddenly, she felt again the sharp edge of the knife blade on her neck. The sour smell of *his* breath. The steering wheel slippery with blood. Her blood. Her heart pounding so loudly it threatened to push out the windows of the car. She heard herself whimpering, "Don't hurt me, please don't hurt me."

Then she knew. She *had* seen him. It *was* him. Standing in the middle of the street three blocks from her house with a baseball bat in his hands. The same bat he had used to break her arms.

He'd finally come to get her.

CHAPTER FIVE

He stood frozen and stared into the car until a few seconds later when the car sped away. Disbelieving, he stared in amazement as the red taillights of the sleek low-slung Thunderbird with its custom hood ornament disappeared around the corner a few blocks away. Suddenly, he heard voices — police, looking for him.

Scrambling up a gently sloping lawn, he cut between two tall houses. He ran until he came to a chain-link gate which he vaulted over without breaking his stride. He half-ran, half-stumbled through a shadowy back yard and finally found himself in a dark alley. His breath ragged, he drew in huge gulps as he opened the sagging door of a tumbled down brick garage. Flattening himself against the wall of the garage, he brushed at cobwebs.

He stayed motionless, trying not to sneeze as he heard footsteps pounding within a few feet of him. He felt certain that at any moment the door would explode open and a flashlight would blind him but the footsteps faded and finally he could no longer hear voices or footsteps.

Finally he felt safe enough to think about what he had seen in the car that almost ran him down.

It was *her*. The whore who had sent him to jail the last time.

He slowly opened the door of the garage and peered out. He eased the door shut then started walking toward a streetlight at the end of the alley where he found himself on Eighteenth and Race Street. He kept close to the shadows of the buildings, away from the street lights and the few porch lights that some people had left on for late-night stragglers in their households. He wondered if anyone had left a light on for the whore he had seen in the car.

He walked through the night, thinking hard about her. Remembering everything that happened to him since the last time he had seen her.

At Clarkson he turned back toward Colfax and headed for his boardinghouse. The restless street still moved with light traffic. A tired-looking hooker approached him, but he waved her away. He finally reached his room, threw himself into his bed.

The little girl from the zoo and the nurse he had left spread-eagled on the car were forgotten now. The whore, Caroline Jordan, *was* here in Denver. Just as he'd known she would be. And, more importantly, she had practically fallen into his lap. Now all he had to do was find out where she lived and pay her a visit.

CHAPTER SIX

Even upstairs Jane heard the scream — piercing the solid oak floor and reverberating off the brick walls of her studio. She dropped her paintbrush and bolted for her door. The scream trailed away into a moan so desperate and frightened it caused her to stumble down the last two stairs. With an awkward lunge, she grabbed the oak bannister and regained her balance, leaned sideways and looked into the kitchen.

Caroline lay on the floor in front of the sink, her

knees drawn up to her chin. Broken glass was all around her. She was lying in it. Blood streamed from a deep cut on her hand.

"What the hell?" Jane ran to her and lifted her into a sitting position. Cradling Caroline, Jane stroked her hair and rubbed her back. "Easy, baby. Easy. What is it? What's the matter?"

She tried to turn Caroline's face so she could see into Caroline's eyes, but Caroline buried her face in Jane's shoulder and continued to sob. Jane took her hand and saw that the cut was deep.

"Oh God, please, please, don't let him hurt me anymore. Don't hurt me. I'll do anything. Don't hurt me."

"Honey, it's me. I'm not going to hurt you. Listen to me. We've got to get you to Medi-Quick. This cut's pretty deep."

"No!" Caroline screamed. "I can't go outside. He's out there." She crawled away from Jane and huddled against the sink. "No," she whimpered. Jane saw with alarm that the blood was running freely down Caroline's arm and forming a small puddle on the kitchen floor.

"Okay," Jane soothed her. "Come on. Let's go into the bathroom and get some pressure bandages on that cut."

"Judy said I'd never have to go through with it again," Caroline said nonsensically. "Please don't make me go."

Caroline continued to cry as Jane led her to the bathroom, sounding as though she would never stop, as if the fear and pain were too deep to ever be erased by crying.

* * * * *

Rain had begun sometime in the night. Jane wondered absently if it was cold enough to snow. Even in May, snow was not unusual for Colorado. She looked at the outside thermometer hanging beside the kitchen window; it read 43 degrees. The backyard was flooded, the trees dripped water.

She turned away from the window and busied herself making Red Zinger herbal tea. As she waited for the water to boil in the blue tea kettle, she thought of Matty and Brooke. She felt vaguely guilty for not having checked with Brooke recently about Evie, but she had been totally preoccupied getting ready for the opening of her gallery coming up in August. For months, it had dominated her life. Until last night.

Jane looked at the kitchen clock. Nine o'clock. Caroline had been sleeping nearly five hours. Caroline had been unable to talk because all she could do was cry. Finally, around four in the morning, she had fallen asleep on the couch. Restless, Jane had gone upstairs to her own apartment and selected *Black Widow* from her stock of movies and started to watch it on Caroline's VCR. Sometime after Theresa Russell bumped off Dennis Hopper, Jane had fallen asleep in the large recliner next to the couch where Caroline lay sleeping. She woke to the sound of the rain and thunder around eight-thirty.

Jane dropped two double tea bags into the teapot and sat down while she waited for the tea to steep. She was deeply troubled. She had never seen Caroline act hysterically before. Caroline was as

42

controlled and calm in a crisis as anyone Jane had ever known. Yet last night she appeared to have had an emotional breakdown.

What could have happened that would make her behave this way? Jane knew that Caroline's affairs usually occurred when she was under stress. Three years ago when she had been working on her promotion to associate professor, she had had a brief affair with a woman she met at a conference in Seattle. When Caroline's father had died, Caroline had returned from his funeral in Illinois and immediately had had an affair with another graduate student.

Jane had been stunned and hurt. She had tried to reason with Caroline. She had tried to understand. She had cried and pleaded, but nothing she did or said seemed to have any effect on her. Caroline had calmly assured her that she loved her and had no intention of leaving her. Finally, Jane went to stay with a friend. After three days, Caroline had called her and begged her to come back. And Jane had. Then Caroline had left. During the year they were separated, Jane knew that Caroline had had other lovers. She had hoped that the separation would make Caroline realize how much she loved her and that she couldn't live without her. That much *had* happened. After nine months of living apart, Caroline had called her from Denver one night and said miserably, "I can't stand it." There was a long silence and Caroline whispered, "Will you come here and live?"

"Will you stop sleeping with other people?"

"Is it a condition? Do I have to — to have you?"

"I don't know," Jane admitted.

43

"Can you stand it?"

"No," Jane had groaned. "But I will. If you promise not to ever leave me again."

"*That* I will promise," Caroline had vowed.

And she had kept her promise, Jane thought, sipping her tea and looking out the kitchen window at the rain. They had been together longer than any other couple she knew. And now this. But what was *this?* She didn't know and wouldn't until Caroline woke up.

Jane wondered about the situation with Evie. She remembered how upset Caroline had been at first, but as Evie had improved and finally gotten better, Caroline had seemed to calm down and put it out of her mind. Jane realized with a twinge of alarm that she couldn't think of anything that had happened — and yet she knew her lover had been genuinely traumatized. Usually she and Caroline were in touch enough for her to know, or at least be able to guess, what might be troubling her.

Now it struck her that she and Caroline hadn't actually talked to each other or spent the night together in weeks. And she knew it was for the same reasons she hadn't talked to or seen Brooke, or any of her other friends, except those connected to the gallery, for weeks.

The opening of her gallery in August and Caroline's affair with Susan McKay.

Jane tried to separate the two and couldn't. She had been working at the gallery almost every night for months, and when she wasn't at the gallery, she was drawing or painting in her studio. She'd had

44

numerous meetings with Deidre and Kim, her co-owners, and meetings with bankers and lawyers. When she wasn't working or painting, she was sleeping.

But she hadn't been with Caroline at all.

She had heard the rumors of Caroline's attraction to Susan weeks ago. She had actually seen them together at a softball game and finally, one evening after working late at the gallery, she and Michael had stopped by the Magnolia to have a beer. When Jane saw Caroline's Thunderbird in the parking lot, she was delighted that she would get to see her lover and ride home with her. They could have a drink and maybe even dance together before going home, although Jane had known that Caroline would throw a fit when she saw Jane's paint-spattered, sawdust-covered clothes. As she and Michael had walked into the bar, she saw Caroline and Susan sitting at a table in the back, holding hands and laughing, their heads close together. Only Margaret, standing behind the bar, saw Jane's expectant smile fade and watched as Michael took her firmly by the elbow and guided her back outside.

"You may have to live with it," Michael had told Jane on the way to his car, "but you don't have to look at it."

After that, she had started working even longer hours and avoiding Caroline and the Steel Magnolia. Last night was the first time she had even touched Caroline in over two weeks. She stared out the window into the rain-drenched backyard and felt depression seep into her. She finished her second cup of tea and decided to go check on Caroline. She turned toward the hallway that led to the living room.

Caroline was standing in the doorway. Her face was puffy and her eyes were bloodshot. She wore a long terrycloth robe and a pair of slippers, but she shook as if she were cold.

"I thought you were still asleep!" Jane exclaimed.

Caroline shook her head. "I have to shower and get to work." She walked unsteadily to the counter and leaned against it while she poured herself a cup of tea.

"You don't have to work today," Jane reminded her. "It's Saturday."

Caroline added some honey to her tea. "Good. I have so much work to do. I'll be so glad when finals are over. I have so many exams and papers to grade."

Jane looked at her, disbelieving. "Are you joking?"

"About what?" Caroline asked, looking at her over the rim of her cup.

"Carrie, we need to talk about last night."

"Oh? I didn't think you were interested in talking to me," Caroline said flatly. "You certainly haven't made any attempt to see me or talk to me for weeks."

Jane flushed with anger. "If you were home once in a while, maybe I would talk to you."

"I've been home plenty of times," Caroline countered. "You weren't here."

"So you decided you needed a little company,

huh? Is that what this whole thing is about? I've been neglecting you and so you take up with Susan McKay?"

Caroline stared at her. "Where did you get that idea? From Brooke?"

"Brooke's got nothing to do with it," Jane snapped. "I saw you two at the softball game and then last week I saw you with her at the Magnolia. Sitting there holding hands and giggling like a couple of teenagers." She stood up. "Well, hey," she added sarcastically, "I guess if you think about it, Susan *is* almost a teenager."

"You've been spying on me!" Caroline cried angrily.

"I wasn't spying on you," Jane retorted. "I went in there to drink a beer with Michael after work. I have just as much right to go into the Magnolia as you do."

Caroline sighed. "This isn't doing either of us any good. We've been over this before."

"Yeah? Well, at least you've always been discreet. I don't remember you parading your lovers around the Magnolia before."

"I'm sorry, Janie." Caroline hung her head. "Truly. I shouldn't have done that." She reached out and made Jane sit back down. She remembered dinner with Susan at the Magnolia the night before and flushed with embarrassment.

An uneasy silence hung between them. "Okay," Jane said finally. "That's not what I wanted to talk about anyway." She pointed to Caroline's hand. "Let's talk about that."

Caroline looked at the bandage and flexed her hand. "I cut my hand on a glass last night."

"I thought it needed stitches, but you wouldn't let me take you to Medi-Quick. I did the best I could with butterfly bandages."

"It's fine — you did a good job." Caroline smiled weakly, as if to ease the tension between them. "I love Red Zinger. You were right about getting off coffee. I feel a lot better now. And I really like the taste." As if embarrassed by the inanity of her remark, Caroline turned to look out the window. "Lovely weather we're having, wouldn't you say?"

"Listen, Caroline," Jane said impatiently. "I don't care about the weather. Or your teenage lover. I want to talk to you about last night."

"All right. What do you want to know?"

"Were you with Susan?"

"I thought you didn't want to know about her."

"I don't want to know if you're sleeping with her. I just want to know if you were with her last night and if being with her had anything to do with your being upset."

"Yes. I was with her." Caroline decided not to mention the Magnolia. "We had dinner. Then we went up to her house in Boulder Canyon. We had some wine, talked and then I came home."

"Did something happen on the way home that upset you?" Jane asked.

"Jane, I *would* like to talk to you about it. Really. But not right now — I just can't. I need some time to sort things out."

"About Susan, you mean?" Jane looked at her steadily. "Are you in love with her?"

48

"No," Caroline assured her hurriedly. "Of course not. It's got nothing to do with Susan — not really."

Jane shrugged. "Okay. Fine." She stood up and went to the window. The dreary landscape depressed her even more now. She decided to make one last effort. "Carrie?" she said softly. "Who's Judy?"

Caroline froze.

Jane turned around to look at her. "Last night you said, 'Judy promised I wouldn't have to go through it again.' Through what again? Who's Judy?"

Caroline sat perfectly still, as if the slightest movement would cause her pain. She looked into her teacup and felt her eyes filling with tears again. She knew she had to tell Jane. Not because Jane had trapped her. Because it was necessary to make *him* go away. She knew what had happened last night. She hadn't seen him last night. But the truth was almost as bad.

She had imagined him.

The stress of Evie's attack, the estrangement from Jane, the lack of regular sleep, overwork, the lovemaking with Susan, Susan's story of revenge, the knife in the sink, the shattered glass, the pain of the cut on her hand . . . Caroline looked down at her hand. "I'm freezing. How cold is it?"

"It just might snow. Let's go in the front room," Jane suggested. "I'll build a fire and we can talk."

Caroline settled down on the couch and pulled an afghan around her as she watched Jane build a fire. The flames filled the room with light and warmth.

Settled at the opposite end of the sofa, Jane said, "Okay. Who's Judy?"

Caroline sighed deeply and pulled her robe closer.

"Judy McFarlane. She's an attorney with the Justice Department." She paused. "Anyway, she was when I knew her."

"Justice Department? What's she got to do with you? How did you meet her?"

"You're going to have to be patient here, Jane," Caroline warned. "This is really hard for me."

Jane reached over and patted her knee. "Okay. Just take your time."

Pale gray light filtered in through the curtains, dispelling some of the darkness of the living room, but shadows still lurked in the corner as Caroline began the tale that she had kept from her lover for so long. At first, speaking in a voice so soft that Jane had to lean forward to hear her, she spoke hesitantly.

"When I was finishing my Masters Degree at Southwestern Illinois, I had a boyfriend, Steve Hardy. He was a theater major. One day we had a pretty bad fight. That night I started feeling bad about the fight and went over to the campus theater where he was rehearsing for a play. We talked, straightened everything out, and I went back out to my car. When I got in, a man came up out of the back seat and put a knife to my throat. He told me to drive him to St. Louis or he'd cut my throat. He said he also had a baseball bat and if I crossed him, he'd beat me to death and leave my body by the road."

"Holy Jesus," Jane said softly.

"He was on cocaine, really wired . . . Anyway, he told me he was running from some people he owed money to. He ordered me to drive him to Missouri. He said he was going to St. Louis to get on a barge and go down the Mississippi River to New Orleans."

"Did you take him to St. Louis?"

"No," Caroline said. "We didn't make it that far. After we'd been driving for about an hour, he made me pull off the highway into a cornfield and he raped me. Then he made me drive some more. He was babbling about some people who wanted to kill him because he owed them money for drugs and cocaine. I tried to get him to trust me. I made him think I was sympathetic to his situation. He told me horrible stories about all the people he'd killed. I didn't think the stories were true but he described the killings so vividly . . . I was terrified. And I kept thinking, if he trusted me, maybe he'd let down his guard and I could get away. But he never did. He kept the knife at my throat or in my ribs the whole time.

"Once we stopped for gas and I went into the bathroom — he waited right outside the door. I left a note on a piece of paper towel. Somebody did find it — about three days later. I thought about locking myself in the restroom but there was no lock on the door. Finally, at a stoplight in some little town in western Illinois, I tried to get away."

Caroline began to cry. "After that, he got mad and everything changed. He hit me and then . . . he forced me to . . . go down on him. I threw up on the floor and he rubbed my face in it. He made me pull off into a field, and he sodomized me. It hurt so bad, blood was running down my legs . . ."

Jane reached out and gathered Caroline into her arms. "Stop, baby. Stop it. You don't have to tell me."

Caroline sobbed. "I want to. I have to." She struggled for control and after a minute she stopped crying. "Finally, he stopped the car and told me to drive. We were almost to St. Louis, and he didn't want to drive in the city. He was tired, and the coke was wearing off, he wasn't thinking. He got out of the car and when he did, I locked all the doors."

"Jesus," Jane said.

"Then the car wouldn't start. I couldn't get it started. He started to kick in a window. It was just beginning to get light and we were on the interstate. I jumped out and started running along the highway, on the shoulder. He ran after me and finally caught up with me. He had the baseball bat. He knocked me down, he brought the bat down on both of my arms and broke them. I thought he was going to break all my bones. There were lots of cars going by, some of them were slowing down. He took off running across a field. I don't know how long I lay in the weeds by the road. A truck driver finally stopped and picked me up. He took me to a Highway Patrol station along the highway and they called an ambulance."

Caroline collapsed in Jane's arms. Jane held her, weeping along with Caroline. For a long time, they sat on the couch holding hands. The room seemed to pulsate with the brutality and savagery of Caroline's story. Jane got up and added another log to the fire.

Caroline showered and put on clean sweatpants and a long-sleeved T-shirt. She felt calmer, and even a little hungry. They ate lunch in silence. Jane cleared off the table and then took Caroline's hands in hers.

"First of all, I want you to know that I love you. I don't know why you didn't tell me about this before, but it's okay. I think you're incredibly brave to have gone through a horrible experience like that and survived." She squeezed Caroline's hands. "I don't know what else to say except — I wish it hadn't been you."

"I haven't talked about it for a long time," Caroline said. "But I've been so upset lately. It started when Evie got attacked. When I found out that the man who attacked her broke her arms, I thought, my God, what if it's the same man. I know that's ridiculous but it just reminded me of what he did to me. And then last night, Susan told me this story about some friend of hers getting raped, and I started thinking about everything again."

"Oh, honey, I'm so sorry," Jane said, reaching over to touch her tear-stained face. "You don't have to tell me anything else if you don't want to."

Caroline shook her head. "No, I want to. My parents never let me talk about it. They treated me like I'd been sick with something contagious. They wanted me to just get over it and not talk about it. No one in my family has ever mentioned my rape. I guess I didn't want to talk about it either. I just wanted to kill him. My parents did get me a shrink. He gave me tranquilizers. I used to lay awake at night after the pills wore off and think of all the ways I'd like to kill him if I could. God, I had a thousand feelings at the same time. During my afraid phase, I saw him under every bed."

"What's his name?" Jane said.

"Steckman," Caroline told her softly, as though she were reluctant to even say his name. "Gerald Louis Steckman."

"Where is he now?"

"In the state penitentiary at Joliet, Illinois, for kidnapping. At least that's where he was the last time I talked to Judy McFarlane."

"Did you go to a therapist after this happened?" Jane asked.

"No. You know I used to think I saw him all the time. After it happened. My old Chevy was sitting in the driveway. I couldn't drive it. It reminded me too much of the rape. My Dad completely restored it after the police were through with it — I mean, Dad tore out the seats and had the carpeting replaced, everything — but I knew, I just knew there were still bloodstains in it. Sometimes at night, I'd look out the window and see it sitting there — like a big metal ghost — like a sunken ship on the bottom of the ocean. I'd see him in the back seat, with the knife, waiting for me to think it was safe again. Sometimes, he'd see me looking at him and laugh and motion for me to come outside." Caroline's voice broke and she started crying again.

Jane took her hands and rubbed them with her own. "Honey, you don't have to talk about it anymore."

Caroline shook her head stubbornly. "I want to. I want you to know."

"Did you tell the psychiatrist about hallucinating — about seeing him in the car?"

"Sure." Caroline laughed bitterly. "Dr. Leonard said two things to me the whole summer. 'Well, hello, Miss Jordan. Won't you have a seat?' And,

'Our time is up for today, Miss Jordan. Next week, we will continue.' Great help, huh?"

"When did they catch this guy Steckman?" Jane asked.

"The end of the summer."

"Did you have to testify at the trial?"

"Yes, it was awful. During the preliminary hearing they asked me questions about my previous sexual experience. How many men had I slept with? Did I like men? Did I ever take money or presents for sex? I couldn't deal with it. I told them I wasn't going to testify."

"What did they do then?" Jane put the poker back in the fireplace rack and sat down beside her. "How did they finally try him for kidnapping?"

"Well, the summer after I finished my Masters I took a job teaching high school in this little town, Clarkedale. All the other teachers were married and everyone had kids. I was slowly going nuts. My boyfriend Steve sometimes came up on weekends but he really didn't want me after the rape. He couldn't handle it."

"Asshole," Jane muttered.

"Well, after the preliminary hearing, the FBI got involved. It's a federal crime to transport someone across state lines for immoral purposes," Caroline said. "So the Justice Department sent a federal prosecutor to talk to me. It was Judy McFarlane. She told me we could get Steckman on federal charges of kidnapping. It carries a potential life sentence. She explained that a new law had been passed that prohibited asking rape victims questions about their previous sexual experiences, and she promised she'd protect me. I said okay."

"Was he convicted?" Jane asked.

"Yes. He got thirty-five years. Judy told me it would be a long time before he got out. But there's always a chance he'll get parole or he'll escape. He said he'd find me and kill me."

Jane put her arms around her lover. "No, they won't let him out. And even if they did, he has no idea where you live. He'd never find you."

"I know," Caroline said slowly. "But sometimes . . ."

"This explains a lot of things, Caroline," Jane said. "Especially now that I think back to when we first met. But it still doesn't tell me why you were so upset last night."

"Susan told me about some woman she knew in college who was raped." She recounted the story. "I guess it was the talk about revenge. Then when I was driving home I thought . . ." She waved her hand. "It doesn't matter. It's ridiculous. He's in prison in Illinois. A thousand miles from here. He'll be there another twenty years."

"I don't understand. You thought you saw him — last night?"

"I was just bone-tired and a little wasted from drinking." Remembering the lovemaking, Caroline looked away from Jane. "I sort of drifted off and the whole thing came back to me. Just like it was happening again."

"You mean here — in the house?" Jane said.

"No. I thought I saw him in the street. I *did* see someone. Hell, I almost ran over him. But it doesn't matter, honey. Believe me. I imagined him. I used to do it all the time. I've repressed the memory for a long time. I've been thinking about Evie a lot — in fact, that's what started Susan talking about the revenge. She wondered if Brooke wanted revenge on the guy — which reminds me, Matty called yesterday and wanted to know if we'd meet them at the Magnolia tonight. I told them I'd check with you and we'd call them today."

"Brooke called me. I told her I'd check with you. Do you want to go? Are you sure you're up for it?"

"Yes," Caroline assured her. "I'll be fine. I really would like to see them."

"Why don't you try to get some more sleep?" Jane said.

She watched as Caroline pulled the afghan around her shoulders. Then she went to the kitchen to call Brooke.

Brooke sounded excited. "Hey, Janie. The cops just called. There's a break in the case!"

"What happened?"

"I don't know. The police just called and told us to bring Evie downtown right now."

"Are you guys still going to be able to go to the Magnolia tonight?"

"Oh, yeah," Brooke assured her. "I'm sure whatever it is, it won't take all day. Let's say about eight-thirty unless you hear from me otherwise."

Jane went back into the front room. Caroline was sleeping peacefully. Jane pulled off her jeans and slipped under the afghan beside her. Caroline stirred in her sleep and snuggled close to her. She would tell Caroline about Brooke's good news later, she decided. Whatever it was.

* * * * *

"You're a good dancer," Caroline whispered in Jane's ear, hugging her closer. "I knew there was a reason I stayed with you all these years."

"I've been meaning to ask you about that," Jane replied. She pulled away from Caroline. "Why do you think we've stayed together so long?"

The Steel Magnolia was crowded. Women pushed around the pool tables blocking access to the bar where Sandy and two other bartenders tried to keep pace with orders for drinks. In the small room behind the pool tables, another group of women clustered around the pinball and video games. The dance floor was packed with couples swaying to Patsy Cline's "I Fall To Pieces."

Caroline kissed Jane on the mouth. "Because you're the best person I've ever known. I knew it the first time we met. I knew I'd never find anyone as good as you." Nobody ever loved me the way you do. I like the way you love me. Exactly the way I want to be loved. The way I always dreamed somebody would love me."

"Because I'm so romantic?" Jane asked.

"Partly," Caroline said. "But most of all because you love the real me. You know what I mean?"

"Yeah, I do. But . . ." Jane struggled. "What are the things about *me* that you love?"

"Oh, let's see," Caroline said. "I love your sense of humor, even if it is warped, your intelligence, your talent — that certain something." She pinched Jane's bottom. "Besides I know someday you're going to be a famous artist and I want to be around."

"Because I'll be rich?"

"Absolutely," Caroline assured her. "Because

maybe then you'll be able to buy some decent clothes."

Jane looked down at her worn corduroy shirt and faded blue jeans with the ripped knee. "What's wrong with the way I dress? These are clean. I didn't paint in them or anything."

Caroline laughed. "I'm just kidding, honey." She pulled Jane back into her arms. "I didn't fall in love with you because you were a slave to fashion."

"What are the things about me that you don't like?"

"That's a loaded question," Caroline said. "I think you should answer it."

"Okay. I'm a workaholic, I don't pay enough attention to you, I'm jealous of your other lovers . . . need I go on?"

"You don't work any harder than I do, you pay plenty of attention to me, and I know you're jealous but you don't have to be."

"What do you mean?" Jane asked.

"I love you more than anything else in the whole world, Janie. You know that. I've never had another lover that even tempted me to leave you."

"I know." Jane led her back to their table when the song ended. "It's just hard for me sometimes. I'm jealous."

"I know that. I'm sorry."

"Well, I can't pretend to like it. You know that. But I'd rather have it this way than not have you at all." She looked at Caroline. "Don't take this the wrong way, because I'm not upset that you didn't tell me before about the rape. But I've been wondering — how come you waited so long?"

59

Caroline sipped her gin and tonic. "Right after I met you, I was so glad to have you that I didn't want anything to interfere with it. I didn't want you to think that my attraction to you was just because I was so afraid of men."

"Was it?"

"No," Caroline said firmly. "It was definitely you. I'd never been attracted to anyone the way I was to you. When I left Illinois and moved to California, it was a new start for me. I saw that part of my life — the rape and the two years after it — as a dark episode. A bad dream. Meeting you was like waking up from that nightmare. I wanted to put it all behind me. Besides, a lot of people who were important to me had reacted negatively. I couldn't let that happen with you. After I met you and started falling in love with you, I realized I'd never been happy with men. I felt I really was gay. I know what I am. I know what I want. You see?"

Jane nodded.

"I simply wasn't willing to take the chance. And after we'd been together for a while, it sort of faded into the past. I tried to pretend it never happened."

"Well, what you said earlier about not wanting to tell me, when we first met — I see that. I don't blame you for that. Then this thing with Evie happened . . ."

"Yeah," Caroline said. "After it happened, I wanted to kill him. I think I still do. And talking to Susan about it made me remember those feelings."

"I ought to ring her neck," Jane muttered.

"No, it's a good thing I finally dealt with it," Caroline protested. "I'm glad I finally told you."

"Well, I can't imagine you wanting to hurt anyone." Jane signaled for another beer.

Caroline's face hardened. "I could kill him, Jane. If I ever had a chance, believe me, I would."

For the second time in twenty-four hours, Jane saw a side of her lover that she had never seen before. First the hysteria and now a ruthless assertion that she could murder someone. Jane was uncomfortable with these new revelations. She looked anxiously around the bar.

"There's Matty and Brooke," she told Caroline with relief. They embraced their friends and Jane clung to Brooke tightly. As if sensing Jane's need, Brooke held her longer than usual.

"What's the matter?" she whispered.

Jane shook her head. "I'll tell you later."

"Okay," Brooke agreed. "We've got a lot to celebrate. Let's have a drink." She looked down at Jane's torn jeans and faded shirt. "Hey, you didn't have to get dressed up just for us."

"What is this?" Jane cried. "First Caroline gets on me for my clothes. And now you. I'm an artist. We're supposed to look bohemian."

"Yeah, some of you just look shabby," Brooke laughed.

"You look tired, Matty," Caroline said. "Are you getting enough sleep?"

"No." Matty rubbed her eyes with a thumb and forefinger. "I've been working on the long-range budget at work and going to meetings and serving on a task force. Evie's still having nightmares and Brooke is still mad." She looked at Brooke.

"At myself. At the man who attacked Evie."

"She keeps talking about finding him and killing him," Matty said.

"She's right."

Matty looked at Caroline in surprise.

"I can't stop thinking about it," Brooke said. "I'm glad he didn't rape her. But I'm so mad. I'd just like to cut his balls off."

"And now," Matty interrupted, "this nurse getting raped outside the hospital last night."

"What?" Caroline and Jane exclaimed.

"Yeah," Brooke said. She looked over at Jane. "I called Jane this morning and told her about it a little."

"Brooke," Jane said, "you didn't tell me anything, really."

"Some nurse at St. Luke's got raped last night," Brooke began. "Just like Evie in a lot of ways. The guy jumped her in an underground parking lot, beat her up pretty bad and broke both her arms with a baseball bat."

Caroline turned pale. "A baseball bat?" She looked at Jane. "I didn't know he broke Evie's arms with a baseball bat."

"Yeah, didn't we tell you?" Brooke asked.

"No," Caroline said grimly. "I just assumed . . . I don't know. I don't know what I thought."

"Yeah, this asshole carries a bat," Brooke said. "Anyhow, listen to the rest. The police thought it might be the same guy that almost raped Evie." Brooke stopped to take off her jean jacket. "The nurse gave the cops a description of the guy. She got a good look at him. So they did the Identikit thing with the computer enhancer."

Caroline felt like her head was splitting.

"They have this computer program that matches the picture with photos of suspects. So they ran it through, came up with some possible suspects, put them in a photo lineup and the nurse picked him out."

"Did they show the picture to Evie?" Jane asked.

"Yes," Matty broke in. "We went downtown this afternoon and Evie picked the same man out of six or seven photographs. It's him."

Caroline felt the room falling away from her. The music faded, the dancing couples and all the smoke and noise disappeared. All that existed for her was the pounding of her blood inside her splitting skull and Matty's voice. She wasn't aware of Jane's arm around her or her own rapid, shallow breathing.

"And the crazy thing is, the cops had a pretty good idea that it was the same guy even before they showed Evie and the nurse the photos because of the baseball bat he used to break her arms." She made a face. "It's like his trademark or something."

The room became less and less real for Caroline. Part of her was calm and icy while another part threatened to explode. Her head continued to throb. In her mind's eye she saw the man in the street, looking at her through the windshield, brandishing the baseball bat. She involuntarily rubbed her arms, feeling the pain again.

"That's incredible," Jane said in a puzzled voice. She looked at Caroline with a disturbed expression.

"Yeah," Brooke said. "So — we know who he is. We have a name." She clenched her fists. "I'd like to find him and kill the son-of-a-bitch."

"What's his name?" Caroline managed to croak.

"Steckman." Brooke drained the last of the beer

from her glass and set it in front of her. "Gerald Louis Steckman. He's got a list of rapes and assaults a mile long. In fact, he was just paroled from a prison in Illinois. At least that's what I heard the cops telling each other."

At the first mention of his name, Caroline's head had snapped back, as if the name were a blow. "No," she whispered. "No, I don't believe it." She recoiled from Brooke. "They made a mistake. Or you misunderstood the name." The pain from her headache was almost unbearable.

"Holy shit," Jane whispered, disbelieving. "You were right. It's the same guy. The guy in the street last night. She turned to Brooke. "Are you sure about all this?"

"Yeah," Brooke said with a puzzled frown. "Hey, what's the deal? Do you guys know this creep or what?"

"It can't be him," Caroline insisted. Her voice was low and threatening.

"Oh my God," Jane breathed. "I can't believe it. The same guy . . . the one you told me about today."

Caroline stared hard at Brooke, as if she were responsible for her anguish. "You made a mistake."

Brooke looked nervously at Jane. "What's she talking about? What's the deal?"

Jane took hold of Caroline's arm. "Just stay calm, honey."

Caroline stood up suddenly and swayed. Jane grabbed her arm and forced her to sit down. "Don't try to stand up, Carrie. Just sit down and drink this." She pushed Caroline's drink toward her and held it to her lips.

Brooke stared at Jane. She turned to Caroline whose face was white. "Hey, what's going on here? How come you guys know so much?"

Caroline whirled to face Jane. She started to cry. "He's *out*. How could they let him out? How could they do that?"

Although the bar was crowded and the music was loud, people at nearby tables turned to look at them.

Jane patted Caroline's shoulder. "Honey, calm down now."

"Would somebody please explain to me what the hell is going on?" Brooke demanded.

Matty put her hand on Brooke's arm. "Ease back a minute." She moved her chair close to Caroline's and began to rub her back slowly. "It's okay, Carrie. Take your time."

"Do you want to tell them?" Jane asked. "Or do you want me to?"

"You." Caroline buried her face in Matty's shoulder and Matty continued to stroke her soothingly. Jane took a deep breath and repeated the story Caroline had told her that afternoon, including Susan's story.

By the time Jane finished, Caroline was no longer crying. She sat up and wiped her eyes, took a sip of her drink. "I'm okay now. Really. I just lost it for a minute. I can't believe this."

"It's not possible," Brooke said. "I mean, the odds against this happening are *astronomical*."

"But I *saw* him, Brooke," Caroline insisted loudly. "I was driving home last night from Susan's house, and he ran in front of my car. I saw him as clearly as I'm seeing you. Right in my headlights." She suddenly gasped. "Oh my God."

"What?" they all cried in unison.

"What if he saw me too?" Caroline cried, her face contorted in terror.

"How could he see you? You were in the car and he was blinded by your headlights," Brooke said.

"Brooke's right, honey," Jane assured her. "There's no way."

"If he got to the other side of the street and looked in the window he could have seen me." Caroline was approaching hysteria again.

"The odds against that are . . ." Brooke trailed off as they all looked at her. "Sorry, bad choice of words." She pressed her point. "Caroline, he was probably so freaked out by being almost run over by you, he wouldn't have had the presence of mind to look in the car. Anyway, why would he want to?"

"I wish I had run over him," Caroline hissed. "Goddammit, I wish I had. I wish I'd killed him!"

"I'm having a hard time believing this," Matty said. She had been silent during Jane's story and during Brooke's exchange with Jane and Caroline. "I just can't believe that a man who raped Caroline over fifteen years ago, in another state, suddenly turns up in Denver, attacks our daughter, rapes a nurse and just happens to run in front of Caroline's car. For God's sake, it's unbelievable."

"I *saw* him after he raped the nurse," Caroline said stubbornly. "I would know him anywhere. Listen, Gerald Steckman raped me. He broke both my arms, he damn near beat me to death and he tried to do the same thing to Evie and this nurse and he'll do it again if he's not stopped."

"Yeah," Brooke growled. "Right on. The cops don't care. They don't give a shit about it. So a couple of women get raped. So what?"

"Right." Caroline seemed to be in control now. "We have to be the ones to stop it. Rape isn't a problem for men. Unless they're in prison, they don't usually get raped. If they did, they'd do something about it. And they wouldn't ask our help to do it."

"Okay, so he's here in Denver," Matty said. "Why? Why did he come here?"

"You're not suggesting he came here on purpose?" Jane said. "Jesus, Matty, Caroline's upset enough as it is."

"It's okay." Caroline lit a cigarette. "He's from here. He grew up here. It's logical he'd come here. But it's also possible he came here looking for me."

"Why in the hell would you take a job in Denver if you knew he was from here?" Brooke asked, incredulous.

"Because I didn't think it mattered." Caroline exhaled smoke. "I thought he was going to be in jail for thirty-five years, remember? I wasn't going to let him being from Denver keep me from my best job offer."

"You seem pretty calm about the possibility he came here looking for you," Matty observed.

Caroline shrugged. "I'm past being afraid. I've been afraid for fifteen years. Now I'm mad."

"She's right, you know." Brooke poured herself another glass of beer. "Let's take the offensive for once. Have some control over what happens to us."

Jane was confused. "I'm not sure what you're proposing here. Are you saying we should try to find him?"

Caroline and Brooke looked across the table at each other and nodded.

"And then what?" Jane asked logically. "What will you do then?"

"Kill him," Caroline said calmly. "Kill the son-of-a-bitch."

"Don't be ridiculous," Jane said.

"Can I ask a question?" Matty looked around the table. "How are you going to find him? Denver's a big place and none of us are detectives. We don't have the faintest idea how to find someone. He could be anywhere."

Caroline started to object. Matty held up a hand. "And suppose you did, by some miracle, find him. Then what? You say 'Kill him.' Just like that? 'Kill him.' How? How are you going to kill him?"

"Oh, come on, Matty," Brooke grumbled.

"No, I mean it. Do you have some plan? Are you going to stab him, shoot him, gas him? Maybe you could hang him?"

No one spoke for a while. Finally Caroline broke the silence. "You're right, Matty. We haven't thought it through. I have no idea how to go about finding him and I'm not sure how to kill him either." Her voice was hard. "But don't kid yourself. I know I could kill him. There's no doubt in my mind. Besides, we don't have to decide what we're going to do to him right now. We can decide that when we find him. Maybe we can just kidnap him and do what Susan's friends did to the guy who raped their friend."

"Yuck." Brooke made a disgusted face. "Let's not. Let's just shoot him instead."

All at once the absurdity and black humor of the situation struck them all and they laughed.

"Okay, okay," Caroline said finally. "I know it sounds frightening right now. But think about it. We're lesbian feminists. Right?"

They all nodded.

"We're all in agreement that violence against women has got to stop. We've marched in parades, we've signed petitions, we've served on committees, right?"

"Yes, but Carrie, we're not talking about handing out rape information at the Gay Pride March," Matty said. "We're talking about murder . . . which besides being dangerous is also against the law. We could get hurt or arrested. Which brings me to my next very crucial question. Suppose one of us did kill him. Who'd take the rap for it? Do we all confess and all go to jail? What happens to Evie if I go to jail?" She turned to Brooke. "Do you want my mother to raise her?"

"God forbid," Brooke muttered.

"Well?" Matty looked around at her three friends.

"We're not going to get caught," Caroline said, her voice hard and flat. "And even if we did, no jury would convict us."

"Okay," Jane interrupted them. "I agree we could try to find him. But this killing business, I'm not in favor of that at all."

Caroline turned to face Matty. "Well, what do you say, Matty? You remember what your daughter looked like afterwards. Are you really worried about getting caught? Do you really think any jury would convict us anyway if we did kill him?"

Matty sat, as if thinking about Evie after the attack, her split lips and broken bones. A rush of grief and anger charged her words. "I'm for it, too," she said firmly. "At least trying to find him."

Caroline turned to Brooke.

"Well, you don't have to ask me!" Brooke exclaimed. "I could kill him like a cockroach and scrape him off my shoe."

Jane shook her head while the others laughed. "Brooke, you sure have a way with words."

"All right," Caroline said. "Contrary to what Matty said about us not knowing where to look for Steckman, we do have some idea."

The others waited.

"I saw him last night," Caroline said simply. "In Capitol Hill. And he got Evie in City Park and the nurse in the parking lot at St. Luke's. So let's assume he's living somewhere in Capitol Hill." She paused. "Besides, I think he's there. I can feel it."

"How are we going to do it?" Jane asked, feeling slightly foolish. "I mean, I haven't read a lot of detective novels. Do we just start asking people if they've seen somebody named Steckman?"

Caroline thought a moment. "Matty, could you get a picture of him from the cops?"

"I don't know," Matty responded. "I never thought about asking them. I don't know if they'd give it to me."

"Well, don't you have any friends at the cops?" Jane asked. "Surely you know somebody down there."

Matty looked thoughtful. "Yeah, there is this guy . . ." She looked over at Brooke who was glowering. "I could talk to him. He might be able to get me some pictures."

"Okay, well, just try it. But if he balks don't press him. We don't want anyone to suspect anything."

No one spoke for a while.

"Hey, I've got an idea," Brooke said. "Maybe we could hire someone else to kill him."

"Do you have someone in mind?" Jane asked.

Brooke thought a moment. "Actually, I do . . . sort of." She lowered her voice. "You know my brother Jack. He's a head waiter at that restaurant in Aspen?" They all nodded. Jack was Brooke's older brother. Bald, bespectacled and soft-spoken, he was a startling contrast to Brooke.

"Yeah? So?" Jane asked. "You think Jack would do it?"

"No, stupid," Brooke said. "But I think he knows someone who might."

"Oh, come on," Jane exclaimed. "Who would Jack know like that?"

"When I was up there visiting him last winter he was talking about this guy he buys his pot from. He told me this guy is part of some big dope ring in Aspen. The guy's whole family is. And Jack bought some dope from him while I was there. Anyway, he's this huge guy — very spooky. He brought the dope over and didn't say one word during the whole thing. After he left Jack said he'd always been a little afraid of him. He said he heard this guy would kill anybody for fifty bucks."

"Well, how are we going to get in touch with him?" Jane asked. "You'd have to ask Jack and then he'd know what we're planning. Besides, what if he killed us too?"

"Hey, look, you haven't come up with any suggestions yet," Brooke flared. "At least, not any good ones."

"I'm not so sure about this," Jane admitted. "What if we do try to kill him and shoot each other or something?"

"Nobody's mentioned shooting anybody. Let's just think about it for a little while," Caroline suggested. "Take it one step at a time. Let's find him first."

Jane shifted uncomfortably in her chair. She looked into the eyes of her two closest and oldest friends and then into her lover's eyes. They stared back at her, questioning. They seemed like strangers, meeting each other for the first time and uncertain that they liked each other yet. Or trusted each other.

Jane struggled with her feelings. Things were changing faster than she could comprehend. First Caroline's transformation, and now her friends. Their anger was so overpowering, and she loved them so much that she felt compelled to nod and thus commit herself to whatever action they decided upon — no matter how crazy. When Jane nodded, Caroline smiled brilliantly and picked up her glass.

"I propose a toast."

The three women picked up their drinks and waited.

"To revenge." Their glasses clinked. "May it be sweet."

"To revenge," they echoed.

CHAPTER SEVEN

"Do you think it'll work?" Brooke called to Matty from the bathroom where she was brushing her teeth.

"Do I think what will work?" Matty was filing her fingernails as she sat on the edge of the bed.

"The plan we launched tonight. You know, to find Steckman." Brooke appeared in the doorway of the bathroom, toothpaste foaming around her mouth.

Matty shook her head. "I don't know but I'll feel

a lot better when he's locked up." She examined her nails to see if they were short enough yet.

"He never should have been turned loose in the first place," Brooke mumbled around her toothbrush. She disappeared back into the bathroom and Matty could hear her gargling. Then she came back to the doorway. "I wonder how that happened anyway?" She wiped her mouth with a towel. "How could they let someone like him out of prison?"

"Oh, come on, honey." Matty filed a rough edge off her cuticle. "Things like that happen every day."

Brooke removed her bathrobe and hung it on a hook behind the closet door. "Well, anyway it feels good to know we're going to do something instead of wait around until the police get off their butts."

She climbed into bed and turned off the lamp on her nightstand. She heard Matty rustling in the darkness and then felt her slip into bed beside her. Brooke reached out and discovered that Matty had taken off her pajamas.

That's why Matty had been filing her nails. Brooke smiled. It had been a long time. She drew Matty into her arms and kissed her slowly, stroking her back.

"I'll tell you one thing," Matty said as Brooke's hands moved lightly down her hips. "If we hadn't agreed to go along with Caroline, she'd have done it anyway."

"Why do you say that?"

"I just think she would. She's repressed it for so long. I never saw anyone so angry."

"Hmmmm," Brooke murmured, kissing her

shoulder. "I was thinking about that first time we all met at Caroline's apartment. Remember that?"

"Of course I remember it," Matty said, lightly brushing her lips across Brooke's breasts. "It was the first night we made love."

"Yeah," Brooke sighed as Matty's fingernails raked gently over her nipples.

"You were pretty funny in the car on the way back to Boulder that night."

Brooke pushed Matty's hair away from her face so she could kiss her. "Yeah? Why was I funny?"

"You were so scared to tell me you loved me."

"I'd been waiting a long time." Brooke traced Matty's ear with the tip of her tongue. "I was scared. How about you?"

"Oh God," Matty moaned. "I was so attracted to you that night. I'd never thought about you that way before. But when I found out you were gay" she gasped as Brooke slid her hand down her stomach. "I couldn't wait until we got home. I wanted you to make love to me so bad."

Brooke chuckled. "We almost didn't make it into the house." She caressed the soft flesh between Matty's legs and heard her breathing quicken.

"I remember you stopped the car in front of our house," Matty said between Brooke's maddening strokes. "I remember, you stopped the car and kissed me." She bit down on Brooke's smooth, muscled shoulder. "God, it was the sweetest kiss I'd ever had."

"You know what I remember?" Brooke asked as she spread Matty's legs apart and drew her fingers gently through the moistness between her legs.

"I can't talk anymore," Matty whimpered against her mouth.

"Okay, you don't have to." Brooke slid her fingers slowly inside Matty. "Oh, my." She breathed, her own excitement growing. "You have missed me, haven't you?"

Matty ground her hips fiercely against Brooke's hand and began a rhythmic thrusting that Brooke stopped by pulling her hand away.

"Oh, Brooke," Matty cried. "Please don't stop."

Brooke kissed her deeply, exploring Matty's mouth with her tongue. "No, you have to beg me now."

"Please," Matty groaned. "Please, don't stop."

Brooke slipped her fingers deep inside her lover and began to thrust rhythmically in a way that she knew would soon bring her to orgasm. Matty put her hands on Brooke's shoulders and, using them as leverage, pushed herself down on Brooke's fingers. She held Brooke's shoulders tightly, each time pushing down harder and faster.

Matty groaned with the passion of her need and ground her hips hard against Brooke's hand. "Oh, God. It feels so good."

"Come on, baby," Brooke breathed as she pushed deeper and harder with her fingers. "Come on."

"Kiss me." Matty's voice was strained, as she crushed her mouth against her lover's. Their tongues were in each other's mouths as Matty felt herself begin to lose control. She broke away suddenly, her cries muffled against Brooke's shoulder.

Matty lay spent against Brooke, her breathing slowing. "I love you, Brooke. I really do."

Brooke kissed Matty's forehead and smoothed a stray lock away from her mouth. "I know you do, babe. I'm glad."

Matty moved up so she could kiss her, and she slid her hands down Brooke's ribcage to her hips, cupping her buttocks. She squeezed them tightly and then spread them apart with her hands.

"You like that?" she murmured into Brooke's ear, letting her hand wander down into the small hollow at the base of Brooke's spine. Her fingers wandered down further, slipping deeper between Brooke's buttocks.

Brooke moaned in response to Matty's wandering fingertips, arching her back to give Matty easier access.

"Is this what you want, babe?" Matty asked innocently, allowing her finger to slip even lower, probing even deeper. "Is this it?" She made one final move and allowed her finger to slip inside the tight, smooth opening.

"Oh, yeah," Brooke whispered hoarsely. "That's it."

With her finger still inside, Matty gently eased Brooke on top of her and kissed her slowly and deeply. "Good, because it's what I want too."

All the tension and trouble of the past months slid away as they kissed. Brooke realized that, in a way, they had crossed a bridge; they had started over somehow. They were going to be all right. And then she stopped thinking because Matty was doing something to her that didn't allow her to feel and think at the same time.

* * * * *

Caroline lay awake staring at the tree limbs outside the window. Rain still dripped from the branches into the huge puddles under the tree. Her head was nestled on Jane's shoulder, and she knew Jane was sleeping by the heavy rhythm of her breathing. She snuggled closer to her comforting warmth, thinking about her plans for the next day. She planned to finish grading final exams and clean up the house. But next week, she thought, next week, she planned to buy a gun.

CHAPTER EIGHT

"Watch your step," Jane cautioned Gretel Weisman, the reporter from *The Cherry Creek News,* as she opened the door to the gallery. "It's a real mess in here."

She stepped over a pile of wood scraps, pushed aside a paint can and skirted a sawhorse blocking the doorway. "If we can just forge our way to my office, we'll have it made," Jane promised as she bent down to pick up a circular saw lying in their path. "My friend Michael's a real slob," she said as she set the saw on a wobbly table. "But he's a great carpenter. He does all my framing too."

She led Gretel through the large sunny room to the rear of the building. The smell of fresh paint and sawdust followed them into Jane's office. Unlike the main gallery, it was clean and sparsely furnished with a large oak desk, comfortable couch, and coffee table. Jane took a seat behind the desk and motioned Gretel toward the couch. "Have a seat." She watched as Gretel opened her briefcase and removed a small cassette tape recorder, a yellow legal pad, a mechanical pencil and two extra cassettes. When she had everything on the table in front of her, she began the interview. It was the first real publicity for the gallery, and Jane was pleased.

Jane leaned back in her desk chair and appraised the woman from the small weekly paper who had telephoned her two weeks ago to ask if she could interview her on the upcoming opening of her gallery, The Crescent Moon.

"I'm doing a series of articles on local women artists," she had explained in a gravelly, compellingly exotic voice.

Now that she had met Gretel, Jane decided that her exotic voice had only suggested how attractive she was. A slender woman in her mid-thirties, her abundant chestnut hair was streaked with blonde and gathered at the nape of her neck with a tortoise shell comb. Her gray eyes took in everything around her with a cool, measured look. Jane decided she was the kind of woman who was good at finding out things about other people but was herself very private. Her white silk blouse, brown skirt and elegant boots made Jane uncomfortably aware of her own well-worn khaki pants and frayed flannel shirt.

She really is phenomenally attractive, Jane thought, looking appreciatively at her smooth, unblemished skin and full, sensuous mouth.

Gretel said, "I wanted to get some shots of the gallery. I'll come back after you open and do a short follow-up story too."

"Good," Jane responded eagerly. "That'll be really terrific. Great." She told herself to stop babbling, but Gretel's beauty excited and discomfited her.

Gretel looked up expectantly. "Okay, we're ready to go." She pressed the record button.

Gretel seemed unaware of Jane's frank appraisal of her. She was friendly and personable but not, at least that Jane could tell, interested in her. No, idiot, Jane told herself, she's obviously not sitting there thinking about how terrific you'd look with *your* clothes off.

Jane tried to pay attention. "When Crescent Moon opens in August, there will be four women-owned businesses in the block." She spread her hands. "My point is — I believe the women's community is knowledgeable and large enough to support women-owned businesses. And I think it's wonderful that there are women who prefer to do business with other women. That's one reason we're happy to be able to provide women in Denver with another opportunity to support a woman-owned business."

Jane stopped and looked at Gretel shyly. "You should stop me when I start that Chamber of

Commerce talk. My friend Brooke says I have a mouth like a torn jacket."

"Nonsense," Gretel responded, smiling at Jane warmly for the first time. "That's my job. Getting people to talk about themselves."

Jane chuckled and Gretel looked at her curiously. "Did I say something funny?"

"No," Jane said, deciding to take a chance with this beautiful woman. "It's just that . . . when I say I talk about myself too much, you're supposed to say 'Nonsense, I like to hear you talk.' "

Gretel actually blushed, and Jane decided even if the woman wasn't a lesbian, it had been worth it just to see her blush.

"I do like to hear you talk. But that's not why I'm asking you questions." She looked down at her legal pad. "When you say 'women's community,' do you mean the lesbian community, or do you include all women in that term?"

"Absolutely — I include all women. The Guild is not a lesbian organization, though some of the women are lesbians. Why did you think I meant only lesbians?" Her smile was teasing.

"I don't know," Gretel admitted. "I suppose because you're so open about your own lesbianism. You once said . . ." She consulted a notebook she had taken from her briefcase. " 'My art is an attempt to visually express the great and mysterious mind of the Great Earth Mother who decreed in the springtime of lesbian pre-herstory that the world would be ruled by the supreme and chosen sex, woman.' "

Jane stared at Gretel in disbelief and then burst out laughing. "When did I ever say that?"

"It was in *A Different Voice* a couple of years ago. I think they were doing a piece on the Summer Solstice Celebration," Gretel informed her.

"Oh, well that explains it," Jane said, still laughing. "I always have a few too many at the Summer Solstice Celebration. Well, okay, if I said it, I said it." She grew serious. "Lots of my drawings do portray women in strong, loving situations, and I have a series of drawings called 'Women and Myth.' But I draw other things too."

Jane moved a stack of papers on her desk, not looking at Gretel directly. "Is *A Different Voice* part of your regular reading material?"

"Yes, actually. It is." Gretel fiddled with the tape recorder. "I'm a reporter. I read all the newspapers."

"But are you gay?" Jane asked.

"Why do you ask?" Gretel had done something to the tiny tape recorder after Jane had asked her if she was gay.

"Well, you're pretty familiar with my personal life and sexual preference. I just want to know who I'm dealing with here," Jane said. "Are you going to publish this in the newspaper?"

"Do you care?" Gretel asked, ignoring Jane's question about her own lesbianism. "You've already said in a couple of publications I've read that you're a lesbian. You must not care who knows."

"I don't." Jane leaned back in her chair again. "Not really. I mean, I haven't put an ad in *The Denver Post* or *The News* to announce it. But I really don't care who knows I'm gay. I don't have a job that could be threatened by anyone knowing. I do have friends and they have jobs where it would matter if their names were publicly linked with someone who was openly lesbian. Also — my lover is sensitive about it."

"Why?" Gretel asked.

"She's a university professor," Jane explained. "She likes her job."

Jane thought — or hoped — that Gretel was a little disappointed by the news that she had a lover already. Jane was surprised at her reaction to Gretel. She was, as Caroline often accused, "an outrageous flirt." But she had never pursued anyone else with any serious intent. Yet her initial attraction to Gretel was strong and still growing.

"It's different when I do an interview with a gay newspaper," Jane explained. "I mean, I know who the audience is going to be. But for this kind of article, I'd just as soon not focus on the lesbian aspect. I don't really see that it's relevant to the story anyway."

"I won't mention it if you don't want me to," Gretel assured her.

"Thank you," Jane said. "I appreciate it. The point of this gallery is not that it's lesbian. I happen to be a lesbian and some of the women who patronize it will be lesbians, but all women are welcome and we hope they'll come and see what we have."

Gretel put the small recorder back into her briefcase. "Could I see some of your drawings?"

Jane brightened. "Absolutely. I've got some drawings I'm going to show at the opening downstairs in the storeroom." She rummaged through her desk for her keys to the storeroom.

She led Gretel back through the cluttered main room and down a flight of stairs, acutely aware of the intimacy the darkness created and of Gretel's proximity as they walked down the stairs. She could smell her perfume — a faint musk that was intoxicating.

"Are you only showing your work and that of your friends at the gallery?" Gretel asked, turning around to look up at Jane.

"Oh, no" Jane reached in front of Gretel, opened the door at the foot of the stairs and turned on another light that illuminated the contents of the basement. She was close enough now to see the faint dusting of freckles across Gretel's nose. Get a grip on yourself, Jane scolded herself. She wondered if this was what it was like for Caroline. Was she constantly attracted to other women? Jane began to see how hard it might be to resist the temptation with someone as beautiful and provocative as Gretel.

Jane explained the story behind each drawing, and afterward, as they ascended the stairs to wait for the photographer, Jane decided Gretel had definitely relaxed since they first started talking.

"Why do you take notes when everything we said is on tape?" Jane asked, as they climbed the stairs.

"Well, not everything," Gretel reminded her. "I turned the recorder off for a while."

"Yeah, that's right, you did."

When they entered her office again, Jane sat down next to Gretel on the couch and put her arm across the back. "You never did answer my question," Jane pointed out.

"About why I use pencil and paper when I have a tape recorder?" Gretel asked innocently. "Oh, I use the paper to write descriptions of people and rooms. Things that aren't on the tape."

To Jane's disappointment, she began to put away her recorder and tablets. When the table was cleared, she leaned back into the couch. Her smile was no longer merely polite; she looked at Jane directly, a smile playing around the corners of her mouth.

"No, not that question," Jane answered. "The other question. I asked you if you were gay. You deflected it nicely."

"I did, didn't I?" Gretel agreed. She casually tucked a loose strand of hair behind her ear. "I'm very good at it. I've practiced. Besides, I'm the one who's supposed to ask the questions."

"So are you gay or not?" Jane asked bluntly.

"Yes," Gretel said. "How did you know?"

"Lesbians have a certain something. I don't know what it is but I can usually tell. Especially if I'm attracted to her."

"What if you're wrong?" Gretel asked, smiling. She was leaning closer to Jane now, her shoulders snug against Jane's arm.

"I've never actually asked anyone right out — that I wasn't sure about. I don't really know what possessed me."

"Maybe it was the devil." Gretel moved her hand to lightly rest on Jane's leg.

"On the other hand, I've never been this attracted to anyone so quickly or strongly," Jane confessed. "It's pretty amazing."

"Why? Because you have a lover?" Gretel

squeezed Jane's thigh and Jane felt it as an electric shock.

"I guess so. I've been with her for twelve, almost thirteen years and I've hardly looked at another woman."

"I think that's very tender and romantic," Gretel said wistfully, removing her hand. "Your lover is very lucky."

She leaned forward a bit and then they weren't touching at all. Jane was afraid Gretel was going to stand up and she wasn't ready for her to go yet.

"She sleeps with other people," Jane blurted. Gretel looked so startled that Jane felt her face burning with embarrassment. She stood up. "God, that sounded terrible. I don't know what came over me. I'm sorry."

"Sorry?" Gretel leaned back and smoothed her skirt across her lap. "Sorry for what? Sorry that she has other lovers or sorry that you told me?" She paused. "Or sorry that you don't have another lover too?"

Jane thought a moment. "C," she responded. "Before today I would have said A and B. But today, it's definitely C."

Gretel laughed. "Well, why don't you? Have other lovers?" She patted the couch beside her and Jane realized that the conversation, which had been merely playful and flirtatious, was taking a serious turn.

"I don't know," she admitted, sitting down beside Gretel. "I just haven't."

"That's hard to believe." She took Jane's hand, turned it over and gently stroked her palm. "You're a very attractive woman."

"I . . . I don't dress very well."

Gretel laughed again, this time with gusto. "We all have our deficiencies. Besides . . ." She raked her fingernails lightly down Jane's shirtsleeve. "I like flannel, it's very soft and sexy."

Jane cautioned herself to slow down. She had just met Gretel, and they were practically making love on the couch. She reminded herself that Michael could come walking in any minute.

"Anyway," Gretel continued, "I'm very attracted to you too." She reached over and touched Jane's hair. "I like your hair. Do you know you have incredible eyelashes? They're beautiful — so long and thick. And you have a nice body — you look like you're in good condition."

Jane was suddenly reminded of a Bonnie Raitt song "A Little Crime of Passion." She wondered if that's what she and Gretel were headed for — a crime of passion — surrounded by sawhorses, sawdust and power tools.

"Well, I run five miles every morning," Jane said, fighting for control of her emotions. She felt her eyes being drawn inexorably to Gretel's eyes; she liked the frank admiration she found there. I could get in very big trouble here, Jane warned herself. "Very big," she said out loud.

"What?" Gretel asked. "What's very big?"

Only one response came to Jane's mind but she didn't think commenting on the size of Gretel's breasts was advisable at this point.

"Nothing," Jane answered. "Just thinking aloud."

Gretel smiled. "Have you ever considered having another lover?" She touched Jane's cheek softly. "Or would you?"

Jane looked down at the deep swelling curve of Gretel's cleavage, even more delectable now that her hand was raised to Jane's cheek. Her breasts were so beautiful, even under her blouse — Jane's mind staggered at the thought of them loose in her hands.

"Uh, no. I mean, no, I haven't ever considered it. Well, that's not true. She left me in San Diego for a year. She came here and got a job and I stayed there. I did have some other lovers then. Not many though. But we couldn't live without each other so I moved out here. We live in the same house but we don't live together." She grinned impishly. "You can't put any of this in the article."

"You must love her very much," Gretel said softly, moving closer to Jane, so close that Jane could see the gold flecks in her eyes.

"More than anything in the world," Jane responded truthfully. "Otherwise, I'd be crazy to stay with her. I *couldn't* stay with her."

Suddenly Jane wanted to put her arms around this beautiful woman and kiss her. She decided if Gretel moved any closer, she would kiss her.

Gretel stood up abruptly and picked up her briefcase. "Well, if you decide you want to change your ways," she said, taking out a card from her purse and scribbling on the back, "here's my home phone number."

"Don't you live with someone?" Jane asked, looking at the card.

"My lover lives in Baltimore," Gretel explained. "She's doing her internship at a hospital there. It's a long story. Better told over a drink." She came closer and Jane felt her control giving away. Gretel lightly kissed Jane on the cheek and smiled. "Thank you for taking the time to talk to me. The photographer is outside." She turned around at the doorway. "When is the exact date of the opening?"

"August ninth," Jane told her. "You want an invitation?"

"Very much," Gretel said, opening the door. "I want to see this woman who needs to have other lovers when she has you." She winked and then she was gone.

Jane stood motionless for a few minutes. She stared at Gretel's card for a while and then put it in the desk drawer.

"Imagine that," she said to the empty room. "She *likes* flannel." As she headed outside to meet the photographer, she thought back over the interview and marveled at the rapid escalation of her flirtation with Gretel Weisman.

"Way to go, Sellers, this is all you need," she muttered to herself. "Like your life isn't complicated enough."

After the photographer had taken his pictures, Jane went back into the gallery and contemplated the unholy mess that faced her. It reflected the state of her personal life, she decided.

It had been two weeks since she and Caroline had sat in the Steel Magnolia with Matty and Brooke and conspired to track down Gerald Steckman. Since then Matty had talked Bill

McDougall, her cop friend, into giving her mug shots of Steckman from which the women had many copies made. Then, they found, they were stymied.

"We still don't know where to start," Matty had complained the previous weekend.

"Maybe we could hire someone to find him," Brooke suggested.

"Yeah?" Jane challenged. "Like who?"

"Yeah, where're Kate Delafield or Caitlin Reese when we need them?" Brooke grumbled.

"Who?" Matty asked. "Who are they?"

"Never mind," Brooke said. "You never read anything but reports and journals."

"Well, we could show his picture to people in the area where we think he lives," Caroline had suggested.

"That'll take forever," Jane said. "And it's dangerous. Besides, if we keep asking questions about Steckman, eventually the police will get wind of it. I don't think they'll like the fact that we've been trying to find this guy. Maybe we should just let them do their job. They have more manpower anyway."

"Yeah, well, we have womanpower," Brooke said half-heartedly.

By the end of the evening, they still had not decided on a strategy to find Steckman. Nothing had really changed except that now, in addition to all their other responsibilities, they were hunting down a rapist. But they didn't know where to look.

Caroline was still seeing Susan McKay. Jane was still working late nights at the gallery. The only thing that had changed, Jane thought wistfully, was that now she wouldn't have to spend a lot of lonely nights at the gallery working. She could, if she wanted, spend her nights curled up with Gretel Weisman, with whom she had something in common: they both had other lovers. She assumed that Gretel's relationship with her intern in Baltimore was serious and long-term — otherwise why mention it at all?

Walking to the trashcan in the corner, she bumped her shin on a sawhorse and cursed Michael. If he would just learn to pick up his tools, Jane thought, he'd be almost perfect. She decided to call him later and yell at him about the saw. Then she would ask him to come to dinner with his lover. She and Caroline hadn't seen Michael or Brian socially for a couple of months.

Jane stopped suddenly. "Wait a minute," she whispered aloud. She stood motionless, her mind racing ahead, considering all the possibilities. The longer she thought about it, the more she cursed herself for not having thought of it before. She turned off the lights, locked the door, and went down the street to Yer Burrito, the restaurant owned by her friends, Ruth Williams and Lin Tran.

Ruth was a large black woman with chin-length dreadlocks peppered with gray. With her lover, Lin, a tiny Vietnamese woman, the two enterprising women owned Yer Burrito Is Ready. Everyone kidded them about the incongruity of their ethnic origins and the food they served in their restaurant. Especially Matty.

"Why, in a restaurant owned by a black woman and a Vietnamese woman, can I not get anything but a burrito?" Matty had once complained. "I want down-home Southern food — North Carolina food. Grits, gravy, biscuits, collards, tripe . . ."

Ruth had snorted derisively. "Girl, I'm gonna tell you right now, you the only thing from N.C. that I ever liked at all. That asshole Jessie Helms is enough to make me hope the whole damn state drop into the damn ocean. You eat your burritos and shut your mouth."

During this exchange, Lin had placidly continued to concoct what *The Rocky Mountain News* restaurant critic called "the biggest, hottest, bestest burrito outside of El Paso, and that includes every Tex-Mex hole-in-the-wall from San Antonio to Fort Worth, Texas."

"Hey, woman," Ruth growled at Jane in her most amiable voice, which intimidated most people. "Where you been today? You usually in here four times before now."

"I gotta use the phone," Jane said, rushing into the kitchen and almost bowling over Lin who was coming out with two huge combination platters in her tiny hands.

"You want red or green chili, Jane?" Lin asked.

"Red," Jane said as she dialed the phone. While she waited for Caroline to answer, Jane watched Lin ladle generous amounts of red chili over her burrito. Her mouth began to water.

"You tell Caroline to get her pretty behind down here before her food gets cold," Ruth said gruffly. Jane smiled to herself. Caroline was the only person Jane had ever seen Ruth be civil to, except for Lin.

94

"Hi, honey," she said to Caroline. "What're you doing?"

"Jane," Caroline said sternly. "I was on a chair vacuuming cobwebs in the living room. This better be important — I almost broke my leg getting to the phone."

"Well, you tell me if you think it's important. I may have figured out a solution to our problem of trying to find . . ." She lowered her voice, "You-know-who."

"Steckman?" Caroline breathed.

"Yes," Jane said. "I think I know how we can do it."

There was a brief silence, then Caroline said firmly, "I'll be there in ten minutes. Tell Ruthie I'll have the taco plate."

"Will do." Jane hung up and walked over to Ruthie. "Tuck a few more tacos. She'll be here in ten minutes."

"Huh, I'll tuck your taco in *less* than ten minutes," Ruth threatened and lumbered off to fix Caroline's favorite. Jane settled down and looked at her burrito. She decided that, for once, she wouldn't wait for Caroline and dug into her food with gusto. Then, she would call Michael and Brian, and invite them over tonight.

Several hours later, Jane opened the door and greeted her two friends, taking the pie from Brian and talking to them both over her shoulder.

"Michael, you may go in the front room and relax," Jane said. She motioned to Brian. "You follow me. You can open the bottle of burgundy"

"How did the interview go this afternoon?" Brian asked, extracting the cork from the bottle.

Jane filled four glasses with burgundy. "Terrific. The woman who interviewed me was named Gretel Weisman."

"Is she cute?" Brian asked.

"Very." Jane smiled fleetingly. "In the extreme."

"Hmm," Brian said impishly. "How extreme?"

Jane pushed him in the direction of the living room. "We'll talk about it later."

Jane put the wine glasses and bottle on a tray and joined Michael in the living room. Brian set the tray down on the coffee table in front of the fireplace.

"Where's Caroline?" Michael asked.

"Right here," Caroline said as she came into the room. "Sorry. I'm running late. Just got out of the shower."

"Jane was just telling us how the woman reporter who interviewed her today seduced her at the gallery," Brian teased, glancing over at Jane who immediately choked on her wine.

"Baby!" Caroline exclaimed, patting her on the back. "What's the matter?"

"Nothing," Jane said, red-faced and sputtering. "God, Brian, do you have to lie all the time?"

"His mother says when he was a little boy, he lied when the truth was easier," Michael quipped.

Brian looked at Jane curiously, unaware of how close to the truth he had been.

"Well, I'm not at all surprised," Caroline said, still patting Jane's back. "These famous artists lead very exciting lives."

"I'm an artist, too. Why does no one ever want to interview me?" Brian asked.

"You call stuffing wolverines art?" Michael kidded.

"You were pretty impressed the first time you saw me with my wolverine," Brian reminded him.

Brian Redman was an unflappable young man with humorous brown eyes and the compact body of a gymnast, which he had been in college. His unfailing good humor, sometimes on the bizarre side, provided a contrast to Michael's more sober, conservative nature. Brian worked as a curator at the Denver Museum of Natural History which was where he had met Michael one rainy Saturday three years before.

"Don't let anyone ever tell you that Michael is not a smooth mover," Brian once told him. "I was working on an exhibit on the third floor . . . the Native American section. I was trying to get this damned stuffed wolverine to sit up but it kept falling over. Suddenly, I look up and there's this sodden man staring at me, dripping water all over the floor. He clears his throat and I'm waiting, right? Because I can't wait to hear what this guy is going to say to me while I'm trying to get this wolverine to sit up. So he says, 'That's a lovely beaver you have there. Perhaps if you stuck a metal rod up its ass it would stand up better.' I knew right then I was in love."

Both men were absorbed in their work, devoted to each other and, Jane thought fondly as she watched them kidding each other, they were reliable friends.

"First of all," Jane said, "I want you to tell Caroline what you told me about the drag queen who got killed, Bri. Remember? When you were on the board at the Gay Community Center?"

Brian frowned. "You mean the one who pulled the scissors on the cop?"

"Yes," Jane agreed. "Remember? Right after that happened you told me about it. You were on the Task Force that investigated it for the Center, right?" She nodded at Caroline. "I just want Caroline to hear it."

"Okay," Brian said, setting his wine glass on the coffee table. "You remember the male prostitute that the cops shot last spring? He allegedly ran while they were trying to arrest him. They chased him into an alley, had him cornered. Then the cops said he pulled a knife on them and so they shot him." Brian shook his head. "It was ridiculous. But what wasn't in the papers was that this guy was really a transvestite. He had already had the breast implants and was in the final stages of the big change when he got shot."

"Whoa." Caroline stopped him. "What's the 'big change?' "

"Sex change," Michael informed her. "Jeez, even I know that."

"Like a transsexual?" Caroline asked.

"Yeah. This is all irrelevant except to say that he was a little emotionally stressed and *not* strung out on crack like the papers said. The operations themselves are pretty physically debilitating. I have no idea why — or even how — this guy was out on the street. But, independent of that, we also found out that his 'knife' the cops say he pulled on them was a pair of *scissors.*" He snorted. "Come on, who's driving? A panicky transsexual pulls a pair of manicure scissors from his purse and the cops blow him away?"

Brian shook his head again and poured himself another glass of wine. "Get real."

"Oh, I think I remember that story now," Caroline said. "Didn't the police and paramedics refuse to touch the guy's body because they were afraid he had AIDS?"

"It was the first one reported," Michael said bitterly.

"Tell Caroline what else you told me," Jane prompted. "About how you found out what really happened that night."

"It was really something," Brian said. "That night we had some kind of meeting at the Center. I think it was the AIDS Hotline network or something. Anyway, afterwards some of us went down to a new bar just off Colfax on Pearl Street to have a couple of beers. Just after midnight all these drag queens and whores came running in and started screaming about the shooting. It was unbelievable."

Caroline looked puzzled. "Yeah? So?"

"Just that these people already knew what had happened. The network of information on Colfax and Broadway is phenomenal. Street people know everything and they know it before anybody else."

Caroline looked at Jane, understanding beginning to show on her face.

"The truly amazing thing," Michael interjected, "is that Brian says most of what the street people told him that night held up when GCC did their own investigation later on."

"I'll bet you met a lot of interesting people when you worked at the Center," Caroline prompted.

"That's true," Brian agreed. "Not only did I feel like I was contributing something to the community as a whole but I also gained a lot myself. I never really understood . . . well, I never understood about a lot of things before."

"What kinds of things?" Caroline asked.

"Well, the Center has an AIDS screening clinic and a lot of people came in for that. Plus they have Legal Aid down there on Thursday and Friday and some of the male prostitutes and drag queens would come in and get free legal help." Brian sighed. "It's very sad. AIDS has really hit them hard. And nobody really cares about them. You can get lots of sympathy for a little six-year-old kid who's been infected from a blood transfusion, but try getting sympathy for a thirty-year-old drag queen who doesn't even know how he got infected — maybe a needle, maybe sex with someone. I mean, you may not understand why people do the things they do, but they're still human beings. And they're still lonely, sick and dying."

"I'll bet it really was depressing," Caroline sympathized.

"It was depressing in a way," Brian agreed. "And you know everyone, even gays, kind of look down on them — the male prostitutes and drag queens. But most of them, at least the ones I met, were fine people."

Caroline nodded and patted his hand. She turned to Jane. "I think I see what you're getting at now."

Michael stretched his legs toward the fireplace. "Well, that's dandy. But I don't. Why do you two want to know about drag queens and male prostitutes on Colfax?"

Jane and Caroline looked at each other.

"Do you want to tell him or should I?" Jane asked.

Caroline stood up and picked up the empty wine bottle. "Why don't you start and I'll get some more wine. Then if you get tired — I'll take over." She looked down at Michael and Brian. "It's a long story."

After Brian and Michael left, Jane stood at the sink washing the wine glasses. She was exuberant. "So, what do you think?" she asked Caroline, who was drying the glasses and putting them away.

"It was a great idea. Really great."

"Mike and Brian seemed to be pretty enthusiastic about the idea too. Sympathetic to what we want to do. I think they'll do their best to put the word out to their friends. Pass Steckman's photograph around. And they won't tell the cops about it either." She paused. I hope you weren't upset talking about the rape again. It must be a shock after all these years to have to think and talk about it so much now."

"No," Caroline said. "It's all right. It feels good to talk about it after keeping it suppressed for so long." She finished the last glass and shut the cupboard door. "We need to tell Matty and Brooke."

"Yeah, I'll call them first thing tomorrow," Jane promised.

Caroline leaned against the sink and eyed her lover curiously. "So the interview went well this afternoon? You were so excited about Michael and Brian helping us that you didn't even mention it."

Jane continued to wipe the counter. "It went well. It was fun."

"Yeah?" Caroline asked. "So the woman reporter was pretty cute, huh?" She was merely teasing, Jane could tell, but somehow the question irritated her.

"Yeah, she was." Jane turned her back to her.

"So? Tell me. Did she think you were cute?"

"I don't know," Jane said shortly, avoiding looking at her. "I didn't ask her."

"Did you flirt with her?" Caroline asked, gently punching her arm.

Jane threw down the dishcloth impatiently. "What is this? The third degree?"

Caroling blinked in surprise. "No, honey. I was just kidding."

Jane looked into her eyes and saw the surprise and hurt. She hung the dishcloth on the rack and turned to Caroline. "I'm sorry, Carrie. I'm really tired."

"I know you are, baby." Caroline put her arms around her and drew her to her. "Will you sleep with me tonight?"

"Okay. But I don't think I'll be much good to you tonight. I'm whipped."

"I don't care about that," Caroline assured her. "I just want to be close to you." She kissed her lightly on the cheek. Jane turned off the kitchen light and followed Caroline down the hall into Caroline's bedroom.

"Janie, I'm really puzzled . . . Why are you so touchy about the interview?" Caroline asked as she turned down the bedspread. She glanced at Jane

102

who was taking off her jeans. "You can tell me. Really. I won't be mad." She examined her lover's face carefully. "Were you . . . did you really seduce her in the gallery? Is that why you had such a strong reaction to Brian's comment?"

Jane began to button up her jeans again. "Look, I don't want to talk about this. I can't believe you, of all people, would be grilling me about this! I'm going upstairs."

Caroline caught her arm and then pulled her over to the bed. "I'm not grilling you. Come on, Janie. I never lie to you. Just tell me. What's going on? Did you seduce this woman?"

"Of course not!" Jane exclaimed. "Don't you know me any better than that?"

"I thought I did."

"And anyway, suppose I had seduced her? Why would you want to know? Do you want details or something? Do you want the chance to play the betrayed lover? Isn't it little late for that?"

Caroline sighed and looked at the floor. "I guess I deserve that. But no, I just . . . Are you attracted to her or is this punishment for Susan?"

Jane shook her head. "No, it's not punishment." She exhaled forcefully. "Okay. I was attracted to her. Very much. It puzzled me. I don't know. I feel funny about it."

"Well, what happened?"

"Nothing happened. We liked each other . . ."

"Obviously something happened. Do you want to see her again? Is that it?"

"I don't know," Jane admitted. She began taking off her jeans again and let them fall to the floor. "I mean, I guess I do. I thought I did."

"Hmm," Caroline murmured thoughtful. "Well, I can't say I'm surprised. I actually expected it sooner."

"Well, what happens now?" Jane went into the bathroom and began to brush her teeth.

"Nothing." Caroline came up behind her and put her arms around her. "I'm jealous. I don't like it. But that's my problem."

Jane rinsed her mouth and turned around to kiss her nose. "I wouldn't worry about it too much if I were you. I'm so busy, I barely have time to eat and sleep, let alone have an affair."

Caroline watched her go into the bedroom and crawl into bed. She felt a pang of sadness and regret. But she pushed the feelings aside and turned off the light before she removed her clothes and climbed into bed with Jane.

She was busy too. Tomorrow she intended to take the gun she had bought the day before and practice shooting it until she could hit the targets she had bought. She wanted to be sure she could hit the heart with some degree of accuracy before she found Gerald Steckman.

She thought about the gun and the way it felt in her hand. She was glad Jane had thought of a way that they might find him. She had been frightened for a long time and had tried to run away from her fear. But all that was changed now. She had friends; they had a plan; she had the gun. Everything would be fine now.

CHAPTER NINE

He awoke in the early afternoon. He walked to the window and saw people walking along Colfax. His stomach growled. Digging into his pants pockets, he found some bills and a little change that his lousy brother-in-law had given him a couple days ago.

"And don't come around here no more," he had said to Steckman through the back screen door. "Charlene don't like you comin' around here. She says she don't want the kids or the neighbors to know that her brother's an ex-con."

He had wanted to smash his brother-in-law's fat face through the screen. He knew his sister hadn't said those things. But he had needed the money until he got a job. Besides, he couldn't go back to his sister's because the police might be watching her place.

He walked to a McDonald's not far from his boardinghouse and ordered a hamburger, french fries and coffee. He knew he would have to get a job. He couldn't get one at a place like McDonald's though. Too many questions. A bar would be the best place. Just go in, have a few beers, ask the bartender if they needed any help washing the glasses or clearing off tables. After he finished, the bartender would slip him a few bucks. Maybe give him a few beers.

After he had eaten, he walked along Colfax until he came to a bar. Outside the entrance three women in short skirts and blouses unbuttoned to their waists stood together smoking cigarettes. One of them grabbed his arm.

"Hey, honey. You want some action?"

He turned around to look at her. "Ohhhh, honey. Somebody messed up your face."

The other whores laughed. Their laughter followed him into the bar. As he passed the pool table, he put his name on the small chalkboard. He ordered a beer and then turned around to face the pool table. A woman walked up to the bar and sat down on the bar stool beside him. She ordered a Pink Lady.

"Hello, darlin'." Her voice was husky, and her hair was piled high up on her head. She stood close to him, and he could smell her sour breath and the heavy scent of her perfume.

The bartender put his beer down, and he slid a bill across the bar. Turning his attention to the pool table, he sipped the beer slowly. The woman looked at him a moment, shrugged and started talking to another man who had just come in.

When the pool game ended, he walked over to the table and put his quarter in. He selected a heavy pool stick and chalked the end. He arranged the balls in the rack. A slight blond man in a yellow shirt and blue tie came over to him and chalked his own stick.

"Name's Roy. Eight ball okay with you?"

Steckman nodded.

The man named Roy broke. Nothing rolled in and he shrugged. "Still open."

The cue stick felt good in his hands as he lined up on the fourteen ball and deliberately missed. While he waited for Roy to shoot, he ordered another beer. Roy ran the table while his friends called encouragement to him from the booth where they were sitting. After sinking the eight ball, Roy walked over to him and shook his hand sympathetically. "You wasn't warmed up good yet, man. Wanna go again?"

"Sure," Steckman said. "Why not?"

"How 'bout makin' the game more interesting?" Roy asked. "Five dollars?"

"Okay." He drained his beer and watched Roy break and sink two balls before he missed. Steckman chalked his own cue stick and sank four balls before he missed. He walked confidently back to the bar and ordered another beer. He was getting a good buzz now. He believed he shot better pool when he was a little loaded.

The whore was waiting by the bar. "Better watch out, tiger. Roy don't like to be hustled. He might bust your chops for you."

Steckman smiled. "How much for a little company later?"

"Twenty-five," she said.

"Okay," he agreed. He went back to the table where Roy had missed and ran the table. Roy looked at him from across the table where he stood with two of his friends. They were both greasy-haired and wore torn denim jackets.

"Eight ball, corner pocket."

"Go for it, Slick." Roy smiled at his friends.

He lined up the ball carefully and sank the eight ball effortlessly in the corner pocket. He pocketed the five dollars that Roy held out to him and walked back to the bar. He motioned to the whore.

"How 'bout a drink before we go?" she asked.

"Naw." He reached out and pinched her breast savagely.

She knocked his hand away. "You want it rough, sugar, you gonna have to pay more."

"Let's go," he said and picked up his change. When they were outside, the whore grabbed his arm. "Let's go over here and smoke this number. I like to smoke before I fuck, don't you?"

He didn't hear them when they entered the alley from the back door of the bar. The whore was firing up the joint when Roy came up behind him and shoved him to the ground. He jumped up and reached in his boot for the razor he always carried but Roy's two friends grabbed him before he could pull it out. Roy went through his pockets, took all his money and then found the razor.

"A razor, huh? You musta been in the joint." He put the razor against Steckman's cheek and neatly sliced him. Then he grabbed his hair and ripped his head back.

"Don't fuck with people you don't know, Slick," he growled. He smashed his fist into his nose. "Don't come back here." He nodded at the two men who let him drop to the ground. Then he turned to the whore.

"He didn't have twenty-five, baby. He was plannin' on a freebie. Ain't you glad we caught him before you did all that work for nothin'?" They all laughed at the joke and then their footsteps died away. It was quiet.

The pavement was cold and hard against his face. The pain in his head and stomach was excruciating. He struggled to sit up and wipe the blood from his nose. Something crunched in his nose, and tears rolled down his cheeks. He leaned back against the brick wall, holding his stomach tightly. He leaned over and threw up most of his dinner and all the beer.

The whore who set him up tonight would be sorry. He would find her alone some night and break every bone in her body.

He reached down and touched the front of his pants. Hard. He knew it would be.

CHAPTER TEN

"Tell me again," Michael said to Brian. "How do they keep it from bulging or falling out of those skimpy outfits?"

Brian sipped his beer and squinted at Michael through the thick pall of cigarette smoke. He turned to look at the beautifully dressed black man dancing on the stage. He wore a huge white-streaked Afro wig that stood out at least two feet from his head. Music blared from speakers on each side of the stage as the man lip-synched the words from a Whitney Houston song.

"That depends," Brian responded. "Some just tuck it up between their butt cheeks and tape it. Some have special harnesses to flatten it out." He looked up at the stage. The song ended, the black man curtsied and walked to the edge of the stage to accept a bill from one of the men sitting in the front row of tables.

"Thank you, sweet thing." The man's voice was deep and husky, and Michael detected the faint shadow of a beard beneath his heavily made-up face.

A new performer strutted out onto the stage, a man in a long Colonial-style dress who was carrying a parasol and fan. As he belted out a Judy Garland tune, Brian smiled. "Of course, some of them eliminate the problem altogether," he said. "Some of them just have it cut off."

As he spoke, the Southern belle on stage unbuttoned her dress and let it drop to the stage floor. Small breasts bounced saucily as she tiptoed across the stage to accept a five-dollar bill from an enormous black man standing in front of the stage. As she bent over to take the bill, the man tried to lean forward and kiss her. She squealed and danced nimbly back to center-stage.

"Cut it off," Michael whispered. His hand had involuntarily gone to his crotch. "That's horrible."

Brian chuckled. "Don't worry, dear. You don't have enough money to pay for the surgery."

"I can't imagine paying to have your dick cut off."

"Plastic surgeons don't work for free," Brian reminded him.

The next performer was a diminutive blonde and Michael could detect no masculine traits, even though they were sitting close to the stage. He raised his eyebrows at Brian. "Nobody's that good. That's a woman."

"That's Clarissa," Brian informed him. "Sugar told me about him. I guess he's sort of neuter now. He lives up above Boulder in the mountains with his mother and his lover. Sugar says it's a very weird scene up there."

"He looks really . . . female," Michael said, watching him twirl a pink feather boa around the shoulder of the large black man who was still standing by the state.

"Yeah, he's pretty convincing," Brian agreed. "Sugar told me he was working in a topless club until a few years ago when they went bottomless and found out he still had his equipment. I guess it was pretty small as equipment goes, but still . . ."

"Who's the big black guy?"

"That's Solomon, Clarissa's lover. Nobody messes with him. He killed a cop who tried to bust Clarissa once. At least, that's what Sugar says."

The song ended and Solomon reached out massive arms to Clarissa and lifted him down from the stage onto a bar stool. Solomon snapped his fingers at the bartender and a drink appeared almost instantly.

"I was at a party once — before I met you — and Clarissa was there," Brian told Michael softly. "He was sitting there on the couch with Solomon eating guacamole dip with one hand and tossing down Quaaludes like they were popcorn with the other. Never saw anything like it."

Michael leaned closer to Brian and lowered his voice. "Have you ever really thought about it? I mean, tried to understand the paradox of this whole scene?"

"Sure," Brian said. "I can understand the drag queens. That's just camp. Everybody enjoys it. Even straight people get off on it."

"Yeah, but why would a man who's gay want to dress up like a woman? More to the point, why would gay men who prefer men to women find other men dressed up like women exciting? I mean, I like *men*. You know, masculine men. Why do they do it?"

"It's more fun, honey," a deep voice said from behind him. Michael looked up to see the black man with the huge Afro wig standing beside him.

Brian smiled and pulled out a chair. "Hey, Sugar. What's shakin'?"

"Me honey — at the idea that men with names like Bush and Dukakis are runnin' for president!" Sugar laughed.

"It's frightening," Michael said.

"Boy, the tips are shitty tonight," Sugar said. "I wish the dykes was here. They tip a lot better than these clowns. Now there's a question you should ask some of your lesbian sisters. How come dykes come in here and scream their heads off over Clarissa and me? I mean those crazy women go ape-shit over this stuff." He shook his head. "You figure it."

"But not all lesbians do," Michael objected. "I know lots of lesbians who think all this is degrading to women."

"They take it too seriously," another voice said. All three men looked up to see a very tall, well-built white man put his huge hand on Sugar's shoulder.

"Hi, baby," Sugar said. "I didn't know you were

here." He turned to Brian and Michael. "This is my man, Steve. He's the bouncer. Ain't he somethin'?"

He was close to seven feet tall and had hands that looked like catcher's mitts. Michael thought there was something vaguely familiar about his face.

"What do you mean, they take it too seriously?" Brian asked, pushing his wire-rimmed glasses up on his nose.

"Well, I think the men who do this kind of work think of it as just that — work. Most of them don't dress like women in their everyday life." He grinned at Sugar. "Of course, there are notable exceptions."

"I don't do it no more, you mean thing," Sugar pouted. "He made me start dressin' in blue jeans and shirts when I'm not workin'. Next thing you know, he'll be makin' me wear penny loafers or some shit."

"I didn't *make* you do anything. I just pointed out that if we intended to socialize only with other queens and their lovers, your passion for women's clothing would be fine. But I want to live in the real world, too. Go to dinner, catch a basketball game."

"Basketball. That's it," Michael interrupted. "I knew I recognized you. You used to play for Tulane."

Steve beamed happily. "Yeah, I did. Back in the early seventies before they dumped the program. How'd you remember?"

"My father's a big basketball fan. I used to watch the games with him all the time. Hey, you were good."

"Are you from New Orleans?" Steve asked.

"No, I'm not. But my family moved to New Orleans from Texas in 1975," Michael said. "My dad

114

worked on the oil rigs. He always followed LSU and Tulane."

"That's where we met," Sugar said. "New Orleans. When Steve was still playing ball. It was so romantic."

"Don't tell me you played basketball too, Shug," Brian chortled.

Sugar's voice dropped back to its normal range. "As a matter of fact, I did. I played guard at Boston English High School." He looked back to Steve. "But I met this gorgeous thing in New Orleans."

"I was in New Orleans on a road trip," Steve explained. "I was playing ball for a semi-pro team in Florida. I hurt a knee my senior year at Tulane. Nobody wanted to take a chance on me in the NBA. Anyway, I'd never been to a drag show — lots of times the guys in the dorm would go down to the Quarter and see them, but I never went. So some of the guys on this semi-pro team said it was a kick." He looked at Sugar. "That's where I met Larry. It was a kick all right. To the heart."

"It was love at first sight," Sugar crooned.

"That *is* romantic," Brian said.

When they finished their drinks, Steve stood up. "I gotta get back to the front door. Break's over." He leaned down and kissed Sugar on the cheek. "See ya later." He turned to Michael and Brian. "Nice to meet you two."

Sugar gazed after him as he walked away. "He's a good man. Y'know, I been with him almost three years now and never screwed nobody else. Course with AIDS, that's probably for the best. I probably never will screw nobody else."

115

Brian said, "I think we better tell Sugar about the favor we were hoping he'd do for us."

"What kinda favor?" Sugar said.

"For some friends," Michael said.

"If it's coke or grass, forget it. Steve don't like me doin' that stuff no more."

"No, no," Brian assured him. "It's nothing like that."

"We're looking for somebody," Michael told him.

"What kinda somebody?" Sugar motioned the waiter to bring him another drink.

"Some lesbian friends of ours have some other friends whose thirteen-year-old daughter was assaulted a couple of months ago," Brian said softly. "Beat her up, broke her arms, tried to rape her. The girl's mother would like to find the guy who did it." He paused. "Before the cops find him."

"They wanna settle their score before the cops get him," Sugar stated. "Well, now I can dig that. But what's it got to do with me?"

"They think he might be living on the Hill," Brian explained. "He raped some other woman around one of the hospitals. And they know he's been seen around Colfax. He might be hanging out up there." Brian reached into his pocket and pulled out an envelope. "Here's a photograph. If you could just look at it and tell me if you've seen him?"

Sugar took the picture and looked at it carefully. Finally he handed it back to Brian. "No, honey. I never seen him. Gotta say, I'm glad too. He's a crazy-lookin' motherfucker."

"Are you sure?" Michael asked. "He could have grown a beard or dyed his hair. You know, to change his looks."

"Honey, I don't think nothin' could make this turkey look any better. Anyway, I ain't seen him. I'm pretty sure." Sugar leaned back in his chair. "I don't get around the streets like I used to. Steve keeps me home. But if I'd seen this guy in here, I'd remember him."

"Well, thanks for looking at the picture," Brian said, obviously disappointed.

"Wait," Sugar said. "Just 'cause I don't know him or ain't seen him, don't mean I don't know somebody who might." He drained his drink and stood up. "I'm on after this. If you wanna know what's happenin' on Colfax, you go talk to Trixie. She hangs out at the Slide most nights. Her pimp's a real bastard though. Be careful. Just tell her Sugar told you to look her up." He hugged Brian and shook hands with Michael, then headed backstage.

Outside the bar, Brian looked at his watch. "We've still got time to go down to this other dive and try to find Trixie."

Michael groaned. "Haven't we played detective enough for one night?" He rubbed his eyes. "My eyes are burning from all that damn smoke."

Brian started to walk west on Colfax toward the Capitol. "Come on, Michael. Where's your sense of adventure? As long as we're down here, we might as well check out this Slide place."

They walked up Colfax past Jerry's Bookstore, Whole Earth Health Food Store, All-Nite Steak House and Bright's Furniture. The black sky above Colfax was neon-studded; traffic was heavy. They stopped to look in a store window at a leather jacket that caught Michael's eye. When they turned around, a young boy with a bad haircut and a girl with

117

rampant acne were blocking their way. They smiled pleasantly and extended pamphlets.

"Hi, are you thinking about Jesus tonight?" the boy asked.

"He's not," Brian said, leafing through the pamphlet. "But I am."

Michael pulled Brian from the window. "Come on, you bozo." He threw his pamphlet into a trash can and steered Brian, who was still reading his, down the street.

They continued on their way up Colfax, passing a man sleeping under a bus stop bench, a drunken man in a cowboy hat haggling with a woman in fluorescent green hotpants, and a group of young Chicanos wearing brightly colored headbands and brandishing spray paint cans. An old woman in a shapeless black coat was going through a trashcan in McDonald's parking lot. Outside the entrance to the Slide, two men exchanged harmless drunken blows while a fat woman in purple stretch pants looked on.

"Boy, this has really been an uplifting experience so far," Michael marveled as the woman aimed a half-hearted kick at one of the men. "We should do this more often."

"We're doing this as a favor to Jane and Caroline," Brian reminded him.

He opened the door to the bar and found himself at the top of an enormous slide that disappeared into darkness. Music and loud voices drifted up from the blackness and Brian looked at Michael gleefully.

"Hence the name Slide," he said.

"No way, Redman." Michael shook his head. "No way."

"Oh, come on, Michael. Be a sport. It'll be fun."

"Are you kidding? How do we know what's down there at the bottom? A vat of hot oil. Some sweaty iron-freak waiting with open arms."

"Oh, you're so boring sometimes." Brian climbed up on the slide. "What the hell is an iron-freak, anyway?"

Michael looked sheepish. "I think it's a guy who pumps iron a lot. I heard some people in the other bar call this big sweaty muscle-bound guy that."

"Iron-freak," Brian mused. "Well, here goes. I can't wait. Boy, I hope it's hot oil."

Michael watched as Brian pushed himself into the darkness and disappeared. For a few moments the music and loud voices from below stopped and then he heard muffled cheers and applause. Finally Brian's face appeared out of the darkness below. "Come on down. It's fun. No hot oil or iron-freak though."

Michael tentatively scooted down the slide, bracing himself as he went to keep from really sliding. When he reached the bottom, he was greeted by boos and hisses from the patrons of the bar.

"See, they think you're boring too." Brian led Michael to a table. "Gee, this place doesn't look that rough." He ordered two beers from a surly-looking waitress.

"Just because prostitutes hang out here doesn't mean it's rough," Michael pointed out. "I mean, they're at the Ramada Inn too."

"Yeah, I guess that's true. But this isn't the Ramada Inn."

When their waitress finally brought their beers back fifteen minutes later, Brian handed her a five-dollar bill and she walked away without giving him any change. "Two-fifty for a beer?" He raised his hand to the departing waitress. "Could we have some glasses, please?"

The waitress glanced back and shook her head.

"I guess that means no," Michael said, laughing. "Now, how are we supposed to find this Trixie character?"

"I'll ask the bartender," Brian volunteered.

After a brief conversation with the bartender, Brian went into the men's room. Michael sipped his beer slowly. He watched a woman with a beehive hairdo of amazing height walk over to the bartender and then look over in Michael's direction. She sauntered over and looked down at him as if he were the remains of a messy dinner. She wore red high-heeled shoes, a tight orange knit skirt and a white tube top.

"Bartender says you're lookin' for Trixie," the woman said suspiciously.

"Are you Trixie?" Michael asked, pulling out a chair.

"Who wants to know?" She lit a cigarette and pulled the chair the rest of the way out with her foot.

"My name is Michael Young." He saw Brian approaching and stood up. "And this is my friend, Brian Redman. We want to ask you some questions if you don't mind."

"We have a mutual friend," Brian told her. "Larry — I mean Sugar Cane said to tell you he sent us."

Trixie's unfriendly features suddenly broke into a warm smile. "Sugar? How is that girl? Oh, God —

it's been a long time since I've seen her. She still got that basketball player?"

"Yes, she's still with the basketball player."

"Sugar and me used to trick down on Broadway. Before it got so sleazy. She used to bitch and moan about that basketball player. 'He knew what I was like before. He knew I like to get dressed up pretty and prance.' Well, I hope they're happy. God knows we could use some happiness in the world." She stopped and raised her plucked eyebrows at Michael. "Hey, if we're gonna talk I need twenty-five bucks. My time's valuable. My pimp gets unhappy if I just sit and talk."

Brian looked at Michael who shrugged and opened his wallet and handed the woman a twenty and a five.

She put the bills down the front of her tube top and smiled. "Hey, as long as we're gettin' acquainted, I might as well have a drink." She lowered her voice. "The people in here get nervous if nobody buys me a drink. How 'bout it?"

Michael sighed. "What're you drinking?"

"I'll have a Pink Lady," Trixie told their waitress who was still scowling. "And Barbara — I want it tonight so move your fat ass."

The waitress gave Trixie the finger. "You must be hard up, Trix — lettin' these two fruit flies buy you drinks." She slouched away, wiping her nose on her apron.

"Isn't she just the nastiest old thing you ever did run into?" Trixie shook her head in disgust. "And that's not the worst part. You just check her neck if she ever comes back over here."

Brian choked on his beer. Trixie reached over and pounded him on the back a few times causing him to spill his beer on his pants. "Your little friend here musta got a look at her neck already," she said sympathetically, pulling out a handkerchief from between her breasts.

"Why doesn't somebody fire her?" Brian asked, dabbing at his pants.

"I think she's fuckin' the bartender. But, who knows?" She shrugged and turned to Michael. "So — why did Sugar sent you two boys to me? Don't get me wrong," she said, holding up her hand. "I got nothing against gays. Live and let live, that's my motto. But I can't figure out your angle. Whaddya want? One of ya gonna do it to me and the other one watch?"

Brian handed back Trixie's handkerchief. "Uh, no." He reached in his jacket pocket and took out the picture of Steckman. He handed it to Trixie. "We'd like to know if you've ever seen this guy."

Trixie glanced at the picture. "You ain't cops are you? I can usually spot cops a mile away. Don't care how long they grow their hair or how scroungy they look. I can tell. I got the nose for it."

"No, we're not cops," Brian assured her. "We want to find this man for some friends of ours. He beat up their daughter."

Trixie shook her head. "No, I don't look for trouble. I got enough problems."

"The girl he assaulted was thirteen," Brian said softly. "He tried to rape her. He broke her arms and her ribs. He's raped some other women too. Our friend wants to find him — before he rapes anybody else."

"Would you just look at the picture?" Michael pleaded. "Please?"

At last Trixie shrugged and picked up the mug shot of Steckman. She looked at it for a few moments and then nodded.

"Yeah, I remember this guy." She drained the last of her drink. "He was in a couple nights ago, maybe three."

"What did he do?" Michael asked excitedly. "Did he say anything to you?"

"Yeah," Trixie laughed. "He said, 'How much?' "

"Did you go home with him?"

"Naw. My boyfriend Roy was in here that night. Roy lost a game of pool to this guy and Roy don't like losin'. So he chased him off. Stupid asshole."

Michael didn't know if she was referring to her boyfriend or to Steckman but he kept still. He wanted her to go on talking.

"Anyway, Roy beat the shit out of him in the alley," Trixie finished.

"Tell us everything you remember about him. What did he have on, what did he say?" Michael took a small spiral notebook from his jacket.

By the time Trixie finished telling them everything she remembered about her encounter with Steckman, she had downed three Pink Ladies and was beginning to slur her words. "I gotta get goin' now fer sure. That pimp of mine'll be in here lookin' for me any minute now. Either him or Roy." She shook her head. "Men are such assholes."

"We appreciate your help a lot," Michael said. He scribbled his phone number on a piece of paper and handed it to her. "In case you think of anything else that might help us find him. If I'm not there just leave a message on the machine."

Trixie took the piece of paper reluctantly. "I don't think he's gonna come back here again. Roy beat him up pretty good." She glanced across to the bar. A man with a greasy black ponytail was watching a pool game. "Thanks for the drinks. Hope you find him."

Michael watched her weave toward the man with the ponytail, and nudged Brian. "I think we should leave now. Let's find the real door and get out of here before ponytail over there takes a dislike to us too."

"Why would he do that?" Brian asked nervously, looking for a door. He finally located one near the men's room and pushed it open. "It's the alley but at least it's outside," he said. He took Michael's arm and they started down the alley to Broadway.

"I don't know why he'd beat us up," Michael said. "Maybe he doesn't like queers. Besides, remember what Trixie said."

"Which pithy bit of wisdom are you referring to?" Brian asked, as they walked down Colfax toward their car. "So much of what she said was memorable."

"Men are assholes."

Brian unlocked the car door. "I'm sure she has more reason to think so than most women."

"I guess we should tell Jane and Caroline what we found out." Michael started the car and pulled out into traffic. "But I don't think it's going to do them much good. If Roy beat up Steckman as bad as Trixie said he did, he probably won't go back. That's all the convincing I'd need."

"Maybe he's the kind of guy who needs more convincing. Maybe he's into pain."

"Well, at least they'll be encouraged to know that somebody saw him. I don't know what they'll do next. I guess that's up to them."

"What do you think about this whole thing?" Brian asked. "Do you think they really have a chance of finding him before the cops?"

"Sure, they do," Michael said. "Tonight proves it."

"What do you think they'll do to him when they find him?"

"I don't want to know that," Michael said forcefully. "But I know one person who won't give up till they do find him."

"Caroline."

"Right. Did you see the look on her face the night we were over there? I've never seen her look like that before. She's always so sweet and warm. I've always thought of her as a Pollyanna."

"She gives that impression," Brian agreed. "But there's steel inside."

"Well, she's determined to get this Steckman guy. I say even if the others give up, she'll stick with it till the end."

Brian looked out the window at the dark streets. "Yeah, I think you're right. But I'm not sure that's such a good thing for her."

CHAPTER ELEVEN

"And this woman — Trixie — is that her name? She saw Steckman in the Slide? She actually talked to him?" Caroline was incredulous.

"Yes," Brian told her.

"I wonder if the cops have talked to Trixie?" Caroline said.

"She didn't mention it to us," Brian said.

"Damn!" Caroline exclaimed. "I wish I could tell Jane. I don't know where she is though. I had to go to Colorado Springs Friday afternoon for a meeting and I didn't get home until late last night."

"She's not at the gallery now," Brian informed her. "I just saw her about an hour ago running down Speer — along the Platte."

"Speer? But that's way off her usual route. She usually runs in Cheesman. I wonder what she was doing down on Speer?"

"I don't know. Anyway, I really appreciate you guys helping us."

"No problem. Hey, listen, get some rest, okay? You looked tired the other night."

"Thanks again, Brian."

Caroline sat down at the breakfast table and looked glumly at the empty driveway, slowly sipping her tea. After a few minutes, she got the White Pages of the phone book.

"Weisbein, Weisberg, Weiserman, Weisman . . . Gretel Weisman." Caroline followed her finger across to the address and read it aloud. "15 Washington." She pushed the phone book aside roughly and slumped down in her chair. "Right off Speer," she mumbled. "Great."

Jane had not mentioned Gretel Weisman since the evening Michael and Brian were over and Caroline had considered the issue dead. Obviously not, Caroline thought.

She knew her jealousy was irrational and unfair. Everything Jane had said to her the night they had talked about it was true. She had no right to say anything about Gretel. Ironically, her own affair had tapered off, as her affairs always did. Lately, Caroline had been thinking about her affairs and the effect they had on her relationship with Jane. She knew how much they hurt Jane; she had intended to tell Jane that she had decided to go back into therapy and figure out why she had so much trouble with monogamy.

Now Jane was apparently having an affair with Gretel.

Caroline's heart began to pound. Questions began to flood into Caroline's mind. Would Jane fall in love with this woman and leave her? Would her own affairs now come back to haunt her?

She would talk to Jane today.

Caroline pulled her car off the narrow dirt road onto the deeply rutted Forest Service access road. She drove as far as possible without getting the Thunderbird so deeply in a hole she would be unable to get out. Even though the map showed the road to be a secondary logging road, and therefore rarely used, and though she had seen no other cars since turning off the main highway, she was cautious.

Unlocking the trunk, she reached under the spare tire for a flannel-wrapped bundle. She picked up a stack of paper profile targets and a staplegun she had borrowed from Jane's toolbox. She would replace it before Jane missed it.

The sun was warm on her shoulders and she breathed the scent of pine and a faint odor of dirt from the road. Insects buzzed and birds called from trees, but otherwise no noise disturbed the quiet mountain scene. She walked down the hill and along a dry, rocky creekbed until she found a dead pine tree where she stapled the first target into the bark.

Caroline walked about twenty feet from the target and removed the flannel covering from the .38

snub-nosed revolver, a good gun for self-protection, or so *A Woman's Guide to Guns* had informed her. She had read the book from cover to cover until she had an idea of what kind of gun she needed. She did not want to act uncertain, thereby giving a salesperson a reason to remember her. The .38 was a good choice — compact, accurate, and small enough to fit in her purse. An automatic might carry more bullets, but Caroline did not want to face Gerald Steckman with a gun that might jam.

She hadn't known if her plan would work. She had dug out an old pair of wire-rimmed granny glasses and found a blonde wig left over from a Halloween party. Over the wig she had tied a large scarf. She had decided she looked different enough, and certainly much older.

She had selected one of the many pawnshops along Broadway. In her purse, she had three hundred and fifty dollars in cash. She was terrified, but she had decided that she didn't really care if she got arrested for killing Steckman. She decided that there was nothing to keep her from at least trying to not get caught.

The pawnbroker barely looked up from the dog-racing form he was reading. Caroline's stomach tensed when he slid the registration forms across the counter. Instead of picking up the pen he offered, she pushed an additional fifty dollars over the purchase price of the gun toward him. To her relief, his eyes hadn't even flickered. He had merely pocketed the money and put the gun in a bag. Now she understood why people like Sarah Brady were concerned about the accessibility of handguns.

If she actually succeeded in killing Steckman, the

police would probably check the sale of new handguns in every pawnshop in the city. But, she thought, the only way the police would ever connect her to the murder was if they found the gun and matched up the bullet in Steckman with her gun. And she had no intention of keeping the gun after she shot him. She'd throw it into the deepest part of Cherry Creek Reservoir. She had already disposed of the wig, scarf, purse and granny glasses.

In a sporting goods store in Boulder, she bought the ammunition. She had also purchased another book that explained various kinds of loads — strange terms like "wad-cutters" and "hollow-points." The book had a diagram of the gun, told how to load and clean it, and gave the basics of shooting. Caroline had memorized the details, then threw both books away.

In her heart, Caroline knew that if she actually killed Steckman, the police would undoubtedly find out about the conspiracy. But, she reasoned, her friends couldn't be held accountable for Steckman's death — they had never actually agreed to *kill* him — only to find him. There was no law against that. She was the one who would do the actual killing. Caroline had finally decided that the odds of the police actually being able to prove that she had killed him, short of catching her in the act, were slim. They might discover that she had been one of his victims and if so, she knew she would be a suspect, especially given her close relationship to Evie and Matty. But, without any hard physical evidence linking her to Steckman's murder, they might suspect she had done it, but they would never be able to prove it. It would all be what the lawyers on TV called "circumstantial evidence."

At any rate, Caroline assured herself, as she squinted into the sunlight at the target on the tree, she had no intention of getting caught.

She stood back about twenty feet from the target and clicked off the safety button. She fired three quick shots in the direction of the target. All three missed. The paper target fluttered in the breeze. She frowned. She hadn't thought it would be this difficult. Moving a little closer to the target, she fired the gun again. This time the bullet at least hit the tree, but nowhere near the profile of the man.

A box of bullets later, Caroline stood sweating in the sun, the smell of cordite hanging in the air, her cotton T-shirt soaked through with sweat, and her arm and shoulders aching from holding the gun steady. But the tattered profile target was punched full of bullet holes.

Caroline smiled as she looked at her handiwork. Six of her last shots had hit near the heart of the target and two others were directly in the head.

As she walked back to the car, she remembered a conversation she had once with a friend in the Army. Caroline had asked her how she had endured the rigors and discipline imposed on her by the Army.

"I actually enjoyed it," her friend had replied, to Carolyn's surprise. "The thing I liked most was the challenge. Obstacle courses, reading maps, using a compass. But the best part of all . . ." She had grinned sheepishly. "And I kind of hate to admit it — was firearms training. Rifle practice. It's such a power trip, you can't believe it. When they put a gun in your hand and teach you to fire, and then you get good at it — it's intoxicating."

Caroline had laughed nervously at the time, her friend's confessions merely confirming her long-held beliefs that guns were abhorrent and would turn even a mild-mannered person into a barbarian. But now she understood what her friend had meant. She did feel different. More competent and powerful. She felt pride in having taught herself a new skill, somehow invincible. Nothing could hurt her now that she had the skill and confidence to use her gun accurately. She promised herself that she would shoot twenty to twenty-five rounds every couple of days or so until she could hit near the heart or head every time.

As she made her way back to the main highway, she thought of the efforts her friends were making to find Gerald Steckman. She was grateful to them and at the same time she knew that nothing they did now mattered at all.

She knew something was going to happen, some kind of confrontation with her rapist. But until then, she vowed, her every waking moment would be devoted to tracking him down and killing him. Because she also knew something else. She had no rational basis for her knowledge, only her instincts. And her instinct told her that Steckman was looking for her too. She felt it.

Caroline was just stepping out of the shower that evening when she heard Jane calling to her from the kitchen. She winced at the soreness and stiffness in her forearm and shoulder muscles. Shooting a gun was hard work, the repetitive motion of loading, holding and shooting the gun involving muscles she didn't even know she had.

"I'm in here," Caroline answered.

Jane pushed open the bathroom door. She was dressed in her work clothes — faded jeans, blue workshirt, and thick-soled workboots. Caroline reached for a towel and wrapped it around herself.

"Hmmmm," Jane murmured appreciatively. "I almost tried something before you put that towel on." She smiled. "I still might."

Caroline picked up her brush. "You look like you could use a shower too."

"Yeah. I thought maybe we could have dinner somewhere."

Caroline continued to brush her hair. "What's the occasion?"

"No occasion. I just thought a quiet dinner with just the two of us might be nice. We haven't done anything together for a long time."

Caroline's heart sank. This was it. Jane was going to tell her about her affair with Gretel Weisman.

"Okay," she said sadly.

Jane unbuttoned her sweat-stained workshirt. "Hey, I'm turning over a new leaf. I'm going to look spiffier. Get me those linen slacks."

"Why the change all of a sudden? I've been trying for years to get you to dress up and eat something besides burritos." Caroline thought bitterly that Gretel Weisman must have something to do with these unexpected changes. Couldn't Jane tell that her behavior was suspect?

"Well," Jane said, as she stepped into the shower and turned on the faucets, "we all have to grow up someday."

Caroline sat down on the toilet lid and turned the brush over in her hands. "Jane, Brian called today. He told me about talking to a woman who had seen Steckman in the bar on Colfax."

"Yeah," Jane said, her voice muffled by the water. "Isn't that great?"

"It is . . . really great."

"You don't sound too happy. What's wrong?"

"Nothing's wrong."

"Something's wrong." Jane stuck her head out from behind the shower curtain. "Don't tell me nothing's wrong. I know you."

Caroline looked at her lover. "Why were you running down on Speer this morning? Brian told me he saw you."

Jane raised her eyebrows. "He told you that?"

"Yes," Caroline cried, suddenly angry. She threw the brush on the floor. "And I know why you were running. You didn't come home last night. You stayed over at Gretel Weisman's house." She began to cry. "And now you're taking me out to dinner so you can tell me you're in love with her."

Jane looked at Caroline in astonishment. She watched her cry in silence for a few moments and then reached over to touch her head.

Jane took an old terrycloth robe from the back of the bathroom door and slipped into it. "I wasn't at Gretel's. I worked late at the gallery with Michael. You were asleep when I got home. I didn't want to wake you. I didn't get up until about nine — you

134

were still asleep then, too. So I went for a ten-mile run this morning."

Caroline wiped her eyes and nose on a corner of the towel she was wearing and looked up at Jane with a tear-streaked face. "You didn't stay with her?" she sniffed.

Jane laughed. "I haven't seen her since the interview." She grew serious. "I've thought about it. I've wanted to see her sometimes — but I haven't. I'm busy. I told you that."

Caroline stood up, put her arms around Jane, and started to cry again. "I was so worried. I thought you'd finally met someone that you'd fallen in love with."

"I have. You," Jane said. "Remember? Even if I slept with her, I'd still love you. Isn't that what you always tell me?"

"I'm not going to sleep with anyone else ever again," Caroline promised. "I'm going back to Kathleen and try to figure it all out. I'm not seeing Susan anymore."

Jane held her tightly. "Carrie, you don't have to say all this stuff. You don't have to feel obligated or scared just because of Gretel. If you want to go see Kathleen, great. I'll go with you if you want."

"Oh, Janie." Caroline took Jane's face in her hands and kissed her. "I love you so much."

Jane grinned. "I love you so much, too."

Caroline put her arms around Jane's neck and whispered, "Would you still like to do something to me?"

"Absolutely." Jane took Caroline's hand and led her to the bed. She slipped out of the terry robe and took Caroline in her arms. Jane kissed her lightly on the forehead and removed Caroline's towel. Brushing the damp hair away from her face, she pressed her lips lightly against Caroline's, drew back and then kissed her deeply. Their mouths crushed fiercely together, they fell onto the bed, holding each other in a passionate embrace.

"God, it's been so long," Caroline whispered against Jane's mouth. Caroline could sense the comfortable merging of her desire and need with Jane's. They lay together, caressing, the intensity of their need coming together. Caroline reached out and put her hand over Jane's breast, fondling it gently. She kissed her lovingly. Their lips and tongues melted together with mutual desire. Caroline drew Jane's mouth to her own breasts, lifting them to her in an offering of shameless abandon. Jane drew each nipple slowly across her front teeth and licked soothingly until Caroline felt a fierce aching sweetness. She groaned with pleasure and Jane caught the sound on her tongue and then stopped it with her mouth.

Caroline was slippery with excitement, and Jane's fingers danced lightly between her legs and then drew wet circles around her nipples. Then she licked the sweetness from each one in turn.

"Oh, yes," Caroline sighed as Jane moved form one breast to the other. "It feels so good. Don't stop."

Caroline pressed her thighs against the soft dampness that was growing between Jane's legs. Jane's hips moved up and down, sliding against Caroline's leg, and she continued to suck gently on her nipples until Caroline's leg was slick.

Caroline moved away from Jane's questing tongue long enough to slip her hand between Jane's body and her own thigh. Jane spread her legs further apart, and Caroline felt a hot tide of pleasure when her fingers parted the coarse patch of hair and rubbed with a delicate motion, thrusting her fingers into the sweet silkiness between Jane's legs. Finally, Caroline pulled Jane on top of her.

"Come up here to me," she whispered. "I want to feel you on top of me." She lifted Jane's head from her breasts, engaging her in a long, probing kiss while her fingers continued their circling and gentle thrusting.

From long experience, Caroline sensed when Jane was about to climax; her hips began to churn and her body started to tremble, and Caroline thrust her fingers deeper and held Jane to her tightly as she cried in the throes of a powerful orgasm.

"Let go, baby. I've got you," Caroline urged as Jane's body shook. She stroked Jane's back and neck soothingly as she felt the strong contractions of Jane's orgasm ebbing now on her fingers. She left her fingers inside Jane until she could no longer feel the tiny waves of pleasure. When Jane finally raised her head and reached up to smooth Caroline's hair away from her eyes, Caroline felt her own tears on her cheek.

"Baby," Jane crooned. "What's the matter?"

Caroline buried her face deep in Jane's neck and sobs racked her body.

"What is it, Carrie? Sweetie? Talk to me."

"Nothing," Caroline cried. "I just feel so afraid. And I love you so much. I feel like . . . when we make love like that, I feel like I'm nothing. It never feels that way with anyone else. And it frightens me."

Jane rocked her gently in her arms. "It's okay, honey. It's okay to feel that way when we make love."

Caroline kissed her lover and smiled through the tears. "I know. I'm glad it feels good. I love to make love to you. I love to be inside you."

They lay close together for a long time, caressing and kissing each other until Caroline felt the sweet seep of excitement spreading through her body like honey in the sun.

Jane buried her hands deep in Caroline's hair and massaged her head with her fingertips. Caroline pulled Jane on top of her and kissed her deeply.

"I want you to make love to me," Caroline said, her voice choked with desire.

Jane lowered her mouth to Caroline's navel and made a slow circle with her tongue before continuing down her stomach to the coarse hair she parted with her fingertips. She moved Caroline's legs far apart, lifted her hips and plunged her tongue deep into the sweet opening. She retraced her way back to Caroline's stomach and flicked at her navel with the tip of her tongue.

Jane reached behind her and found a pillow. She slipped it under Caroline's hips, causing her legs to fall even further apart. Gently gathering the sweet swollen folds of Caroline's labia into her mouth, she murmured her own pleasure. She moved her head up and down, her hands stroking Caroline's breasts while her mouth worked with infinite gentleness.

Caroline felt her legs begin to tremble as Jane increased the rhythm of her stroking.

"Put your fingers in me," Caroline gasped as she started to climax. She grasped Jane's head in her hands, her thighs tightened, and she rocked from side to side, carrying Jane along with her to ecstasy.

Afterwards, Jane lay with her wet face on the inside of Caroline's leg until Caroline pulled her up and kissed her deeply.

"See how good you taste?" Jane asked.

"I want to see how good you taste," Caroline said, lowering her head to Jane's stomach. Jane leaned back into the softness of the bed and watched as Caroline began to make love to her again.

When Jane woke, Caroline was sitting up in bed, smoking a cigarette. Jane reached out and touched her on the arm. "What're you doing, honey? Can't sleep?"

Caroline smiled and stubbed out her cigarette, groaning inwardly again at her sore muscles. "I slept well for a while." She reached over and pulled Jane to her. "Better than I have in a long time, actually." She kissed Jane on the cheek and nuzzled her neck. "I think I just needed you to make love to me."

Jane stroked the silky skin on the inside of her arm. "Anytime."

They lay in silence for a while, savoring the intimacy that their lovemaking had created. After a while, Jane broke their silence.

"So. What shall we do now? About Steckman I

mean? Mike and Brian keep asking around, putting out the word. What do we do?"

"Lots of things," Caroline replied. She sat up straighter and pulled the blanket around her. "I talked to Matty before you got home. She's checking with the Corrections Department in Illinois to see if she can figure out why Steckman got out so soon. I've been trying to get in touch with Judy McFarlane. But so far that's been a dead end. She left the Justice Department about eight years ago."

"Why do you want to talk to her?" Jane asked.

"Just to see if she knows anything. She probably doesn't, but I want to check."

"Okay. What else?"

"Well, Brooke called Jack to see if that guy really would kill somebody." She held up her hand before Jane could protest. "Don't worry. Nobody said that's what we're going to do. We're just covering all the bases — considering all the possibilities."

"I don't like this business of killing him," Jane said. "We don't have the right to decide whether or not he should die. We should let the courts decide that."

Caroline ignored her comment. "Now, to answer your question about what *we're* going to do. I've been thinking. I used to have a cop in one of my classes who was with the Lakewood Homicide Division. I used to talk to him sometimes about his job. He told me once that most crimes aren't solved because of some big dramatic development. You know, like in the movie an eyewitness suddenly comes forward and says I saw the whole thing from a phone booth. He said most crimes are solved by legwork. The cops have this clue — like the guy had a tattoo. So they get a list of all the tattoo parlors and go show his picture to all the tattoo parlor operators. Well, Steckman has a tattoo on his arm."

"Okay, so we go to tattoo parlors and ask about him. I mean, it's possible he's gotten another one.

"And how about this?" Jane rushed ahead. "He's gotta be living somewhere around Capitol. Why don't we go to some of the sleazier hotels and show people his picture? And grocery stores. Doesn't Shirley work at King Soopers up on York and Colfax? I could give her his picture. And doesn't Barbara's kid work at McDonald's on Colfax?"

"Yeah, I think he does," Caroline said. "That's a great idea." She sighed. "We can't cover every place. But we do know some people who live and work in Capitol Hill."

"Doesn't Dana work for the phone company?" Jane asked. "She used to. I think she still does — in billing or records or something. Maybe she could check and see if Steckman had a phone installed. I know it's a long shot but it's a possibility."

"Great, now you're getting the idea," Caroline said. "We can't go through regular channels so we have to think up our own." She smiled and hugged Jane tightly. "You're a genius, honey. Remarkable."

Jane grinned lazily. "I'm remarkable in other departments too."

Caroline slipped her hand between Jane's legs. "Hmm. I know. But I'm afraid I'm going to have to have solid proof of that."

Jane rolled over on top of Caroline and kissed her deeply. "I can prove it right now," she whispered and proceeded to show Caroline how much she loved her.

CHAPTER TWELVE

"You know it's July in Colorado when we start getting this kind of thunderstorm." Caroline watched fat raindrops roll down the window beside the booth where she sat with Jane, Matty and Brooke. The streets and parking lot outside the Steel Magnolia were suddenly illuminated by a bolt of lightning and rain began to sluice the hot asphalt. A deafening crack of thunder drowned out the soft music from the jukebox.

"No." Jane stretched her legs under the table and

picked up her beer glass. "You know it's July when beer begins to taste good again."

"Beer always tastes good," Brooke pointed out.

"No." Caroline looked at Jane's feet. "You know it's July when Jane starts wearing her topsiders *without* socks."

Everyone laughed but Jane. "Hey, would you guys knock it off about my clothes?" She arched her eyebrows at her friends. "Just wait till you see what I'm wearing for the gallery opening."

"Oh, God, don't tell us." Matty put her hand over her mouth in mock astonishment. "Did you buy a *new* pair of khaki pants?"

"Speaking of the gallery," Matty interrupted. "How's it coming? Everything about ready?"

"That's when you really know it's summer," Jane said glumly. "When I start freaking out because it opens in three weeks and I'm not ready yet."

"You told me last week you'd finished the last drawing you needed," Brooke said.

"I'm ready," Jane said. "It's the gallery that's not ready. They brought the wrong carpeting and that slowed down the woodwork that Michael had left." She sighed.

"You're just making up all this work so you don't have to go to any more tattoo parlors with me," Brooke said.

"God, I didn't know there were so many." Jane shook her head in disbelief. "One place we went to was so bad. I thought for sure this guy was going to throw Brooke down on the table and tattoo her whether she wanted it or not."

"Have you guys had any luck at all?"

"Naw," Brooke said dejectedly. "We haven't hit all of them yet but he hasn't been in any of them that we can find."

"How about the grocery stores and McDonald's?"

"No, not so far. Although Barbara's kid thinks he might have waited on him at McDonald's a few weeks ago — he wasn't sure though."

"Did Brian's ex ever come up with anything?" Matty asked.

"He told Brian he might have seen Steckman but he couldn't be sure . . . he sees a lot of people."

"What are these people supposed to do if they do see him? Tie him up until we get there in the Batmobile?" Jane looked at Caroline.

"I told them to just call one of us," Caroline said. "We might not be able to get there in time but it's the only thing I know to do. If they could stall him somehow, that's great but we don't want anybody taking chances."

"Well, I found out some things," Matty offered. "I don't know how much they're going to help us, but I talked to a friend of mine in the Corrections Department. They ran Steckman's name through the computer . . . Brooke was right about what she heard the cops say — Steckman was paroled last January." She stopped and looked at Caroline sympathetically. "I'm sorry, babe."

"Paroled?" Caroline asked in disbelief.

"Yes. They said he was eligible, and they gave it to him. The last the parole board heard of him he was in Chicago. But then he stopped going to his probation officer. So they're looking for him for parole violation too."

144

Caroline's eyes filled with tears. "I'm so glad I went through that damn trial to put him behind bars so they could do this . . . and not just to me but to Evie and that nurse."

"Speaking of the nurse," Brooke interrupted. "I talked to her a couple of days ago."

Jane looked at her in surprise. "You never mentioned it."

"Yeah, I know. I didn't find out very much. I asked the cops if I could talk to her, but they wouldn't give me her phone number. But they did give my name to her and she called me. I went to talk to her. She's a lot better physically, but she's very angry. I think she's mad enough to help us." She held up her hand to ward off the protests. "Don't worry, I didn't ask her to help us or anything."

"Well, what did she have to say?" Caroline asked.

"Not much," Brooke admitted. "I just figured since she was the only other witness who'd seen Steckman, it might be worth a try. She didn't add anything to what we already know. Said he wore a pair of dark pants, dark jacket — he didn't pull a knife or anything. He had a baseball bat — that's what he used to break her arms."

"How's she doing emotionally?" Caroline asked, her voice thin.

"She's having a rough time. Her boyfriend's being an asshole and now she thinks she might be pregnant and she doesn't know if it was Steckman or the asshole boyfriend."

"What a choice!" Matty said disgustedly.

"It doesn't just stop with the rape, you know,"

Caroline raged. "I mean it goes on and on and touches so many other people." She slammed her fist down on the table. "I hate that fucking bastard."

Everyone was stunned into silence. Then Jane reached out and touched Brooke's arm. "Come on, let's me and you go get another pitcher."

"You're still pretty angry," Matty observed after Jane and Brooke left.

Caroline burned with rage. "I am. Aren't you?"

"Yes, I am. But I'm doing everything I can to help catch the guy. I don't know what else I can do. Getting angry doesn't help. It just clouds my judgment." Matty squeezed her hand. "I hope it hasn't clouded yours."

"I'm okay," Caroline muttered, avoiding her friend's eyes.

"When are you guys leaving?" Jane asked Matty, as she set down the fresh pitcher of beer.

"Next Monday," Matty said.

Brooke refilled everyone's glass. "We'll be gone for three weeks. We're going to Disneyworld, the Epcot Center, Sea World — all for Evie's entertainment." She winked at Jane. "And then . . . for the adults, we're going to New Orleans."

"It sounds great." Caroline smiled. "I've always wanted to visit New Orleans."

"Where are Michael and Brian?" Matty said. "I thought they were going to come down tonight."

"Michael's working at his shop tonight," Jane told her. "He's pretty behind with his own work now. Brian's in Peru."

"What in the hell is he doing in Peru?" Brooke asked.

"Looting and plundering sacred grave sites for

146

the museum. At least that's how he described it. He'll be back in a week." Jane turned to Caroline. "Do you get the feeling everyone's deserting you?"

She nodded. "You're even deserting me. You're going to be working at the gallery even more. You probably won't even bother to come home."

"It *does* sound like we're postponing the search for a while," Brooke said uncomfortably. "I feel guilty."

"Don't." Caroline's voice was firm. "I mean it. We've done just about everything we can." She looked around at her friends. "This vacation to Florida and Louisiana — you need it. Evie needs it. Go and have a good time. Don't even think about this." She turned to Jane. "The gallery's the most important thing for you right now. Aside from the fact that we've invested thousands of dollars, your friends are depending on you. It's a new beginning. It deserves all your attention. This ugly mess will still be waiting for us when everything quiets down."

"I'd like to go somewhere with you," Jane said wistfully. "Just the two of us."

"Christmas. When the gallery gets going and it's snowing and cold and people are pushing their cars out of snowbanks and shoveling their walks — we'll go to the Bahamas." Caroline turned to Matty. "How's Evie? She sounded pretty good when I talked to her the other day on the phone."

"Better. She's . . . quieter than she was before this happened. She used to be . . . well, you know Evie. She was energetic and spontaneous. Now she's . . . I don't know . . . she's . . ." Matty looked to Brooke for help.

"She's subdued. More pensive. She's afraid to be

alone . . . especially at night. You know she's always been independent, even when she was little. She seems more clingy now. Less sure about things." Brooke shrugged. "I think she'll get over it — eventually."

"Is she okay with males?" Jane asked.

"Her therapist says she'll probably be uneasy around men, especially ones she doesn't know." Matty glanced at Brooke. "I kind of disagree with Brooke. I don't think she's necessarily more dependent than she used to be. She's just more cautious."

"Carrie?"

The four women looked up at the woman standing by their table.

"R.J.? God, it's been forever." Caroline stood up and hugged the stocky woman with curly dark hair and easy smile.

She smiled brightly at the table of women and turned to Caroline. "That's why I came over. To ask how come you didn't wave at me the other night when I honked at you?"

Caroline frowned. "I don't know what you're talking about, R.J. When?"

"Oh, a couple of nights ago, Thursday I guess. I was drivin' down Colfax about eleven thirty — I saw you walkin' down the street. At about Lafayette and Colfax. I honked and waved and you looked right at me but you didn't wave back."

"Wasn't me," Caroline said lightly. "Somebody who looked like me, I guess."

"No, it was you," R.J. insisted. "You know how come I know?" They waited. "Because you had on your softball jacket from the team we used to play on."

Everyone looked at Caroline curiously. She drank down the rest of her beer and smiled innocently at R.J. Too innocently, Jane thought.

"What can I tell you, babe? It wasn't me. Must've been somebody else who was on the team."

R.J. looked puzzled and then shrugged, smiling. "Well, sure. That must be it. No sweat. Hey, nice to see you all." She bent down and kissed Caroline on the cheek. "Take care, babe. Colfax isn't a good place to be taking a walk." She turned and went back to her table.

Jane stared at Caroline intently. Brooke shrugged. "Who knows? R.J. was probably stoned to the gills and thought she saw Caroline. Next she'll be telling us that Jesus got on her bus."

Everyone laughed and Matty and Brooke got up to dance. When they were out of earshot, Jane turned to Caroline. "She seemed pretty sure that she'd seen you."

"People are sure about a lot of things that they're wrong about." Tension showed on Caroline's face.

"Yeah, sure."

Caroline stubbed out her cigarette. "You know, I'm really tired. I think I'll go home. Matty and Brooke can take you home later."

"No, no. I'll go with you." Jane studied Caroline for a few moments. "It's an interesting question. What would you be doing at eleven-thirty at night walking down Colfax?"

Caroline said nothing. She looked up at Matty

149

and Brooke with relief. "Old dancing shoes still work?"

"I'm a dancin' fool." Brooke leaned Matty back in her arms. "I've got dancing in my blood."

"You've got bats in your belfry," Jane told her.

"We're going home," Caroline said. "I'm very tired." She embraced both women. "You two have a great time at Disneyworld, and that's an order. Give Evie a big hug and kiss for me."

"Yeah, send us a postcard." Jane stood up and shoved her hands deep into her pants pockets. She looked at Brooke uncertainly. "I'll see you tomorrow. Pick you up about eight-thirty." She put her arm around her friend's shoulder and hugged her. "You're helping me, remember?"

Outside, Jane waited while Caroline unlocked the door to the T-bird. The air smelled of warm asphalt after the thunderstorm, and over the mountains, lightning still glowed in the huge thunderheads like hot coals of a dying fire. Jane breathed the fresh air with pleasure. When she slid into the low-slung seat of the T-bird, she looked around. Caroline had finally cleaned her car. "Your car smells funny. I noticed it before when we were driving. Like something burnt."

"Is that right?" Caroline murmured vaguely.

"Yeah, it smells like your clothes did the other day when I did the laundry. It was on your levis and blue T-shirt."

"Hmm,' Caroline responded noncommittally.

"You know what? It smelled familiar . . . like gunpowder. My dad had a pistol and when he'd go out and shoot he'd come home and his clothes smelled like that." She paused. "But that couldn't be, could it? Because you don't have a gun." Caroline kept her eyes on the road. She was silent. "You don't have a gun — do you?" Jane sighed deeply. "It was you — on Colfax. R.J. did see you."

"Yes," Caroline finally responded, her voice flat.

Neither woman spoke for the duration of the trip home. When they pulled into the driveway, Jane finally said, "This is crazy, Caroline."

Caroline got out of the car. "Don't forget to lock your door."

"Are you listening to me?" she said as Caroline unlocked the door to the house.

"I'm listening."

"Well?"

"Well what?" Caroline walked into the house, turning on the lights as she went.

"Caroline, you can't go walking around Colfax at night with a gun, for chrissakes," Jane exploded. "Holy shit, are you nuts?"

"No, I'm not. In fact, I think what I'm doing is very sane. I'm not endangering anyone but myself." Caroline went to the liquor cabinet and poured two fingers of Scotch into a heavy tumbler. "Want a nightcap?"

Jane shook her head and sank down onto the couch.

"Look, obviously our little investigation is not turning up anything. Either we're not doing it right or he's just being careful. Maybe he got smart in jail. I don't know. But I'm not going to let it slide. I'm not going to just forget it. I know the rest of you have important things to do. But you have to understand how I feel." Caroline's voice was fierce.

"He *hurt* me, Janie. He *took* something from me. And one of these nights, if he's still around, I'll find him."

"You never intended for us to find him, did you? You gave us all busy work to keep us occupied while you went out and bought a gun. You could get killed. You could get raped."

"I might get killed," Caroline conceded. "But I won't get raped again. I'll kill him first." She drained her glass. "Or die."

"You need a permit for a gun."

"Not unless someone asks you for it."

"You don't know anything about guns."

"You're wrong."

Jane stood up and paced around the living room. "I can't believe this. What do you think this is?" She stopped and looked at her lover. "Do you think this is a movie where justice will triumph in the end because you're in the right? Life isn't like that. This isn't the movies."

"I know that, Jane. Nothing you can say will change my mind. I'm only sorry about one thing. That I didn't tell you about the gun before." Caroline went to her. "I wanted to trust you. I was just afraid you'd try and stop me."

"What makes you think I won't stop you now?"

Caroline shrugged. "I guess I think you won't because you respect me and what I have to do."

Jane looked up at her. "Caroline . . . can't you understand? Do you hear yourself? We're talking about you killing someone and the very real possibility of you getting hurt or killed. It has nothing to do with respecting each other."

152

"I don't see it that way," Caroline said calmly. "Anyway, it doesn't matter. I have to do it."

"What if I call the police and tell them what you're doing?"

Caroline shook her head. "You wouldn't do that."

Jane sat unmoving for a long time. Finally she sighed. "Yeah. I guess you're right. I wouldn't."

"Thank you."

"Don't thank me. I hate this whole thing. Look what it's done to us — to you. You're not the same person you were. The woman I knew before was non-violent, loving, warm, certainly not capable of murder. Now you're out walking the streets with a gun. What's happening?"

"Retribution," Caroline said harshly. "He hurt me. You'll never know how much. I'm going to kill him."

"I'm frightened." Jane stood up and put her arms around her lover. "I'm afraid for you."

"So am I." Caroline hugged her back.

CHAPTER THIRTEEN

When he first saw her walking in front of him,
he recognized her. He remembered the night of
humiliation in the alley. He remembered his promise
to himself. He would get her and make her pay.

She walked along the street with two other
whores. They were laughing and talking as they
walked down Colfax. He smiled as he thought how
you never saw just one whore. They were always
together. In flocks. He almost laughed. A flock of
whores. He told himself that they were probably

laughing at him. Laughing at him because whores charged money for something that should be free.

He didn't think she would remember him. He'd grown a beard and cut his hair very short since the last time he'd seen her. He'd started wearing sunglasses, even at night, and he thought he looked very different. Most people, he knew, were stupid. Especially pigs, and he knew that the only people dumber than pigs were whores.

He followed the whores for a while, his hands heavy and swollen at his sides. They throbbed when he swung his arms. Six hours inside thick rubber gloves which were submerged in steaming hot water made them swollen and disfigured. He hated the way they felt. But he needed the money from the dishwashing job. His arms and legs were tired. He wanted to go to his boardinghouse with a six-pack of beer, maybe watch television in the lobby for a while. Then go to bed.

But he forgot how tired he was when he saw her. He wanted to be sure she wouldn't recognize him until it was too late. He crossed to the other side of the street and walked quickly to the next stoplight, then crossed back over again so he was walking toward the whores. As he passed them, she looked directly at him. Her face was blank. She didn't remember him. Stupid woman. Stupid. He stepped inside a store entrance once when the whores stopped outside a bar. After a while a man pulled up in a car and the two other women got in. They laughed and waved as they drove away.

She was alone. He smiled and followed her, closing the distance between them. She looked small and stupid in her short skirt and high heels. She wouldn't be able to run in those shoes. When no one else came out of the bar and only a few cars had passed by with no takers, she started to walk again. He followed.

She didn't know he was following her. She was looking down the street. Her face was thick with powder, her lips painted red. She crossed the street again. He followed. When she stopped to light a cigarette by a streetlight, he came up behind her quietly.

"How 'bout a date?" he whispered.

She turned around and strained to look at him in the shadows. "You got money?" She tipped her head. "It's thirty dollars."

"Yeah, I got it." He pulled some money from his jacket pocket and showed her.

"Well, then you're lookin' at your date for tonight, sugar." She laughed a coarse, loud laugh. She took his arm. "I got a room. It's only an extra ten."

"Don't need your room." He pulled on her arm roughly.

"Okay, okay. Don't get physical . . . yet." She laughed again.

They walked along the street toward his boardinghouse. She talked constantly, like she was nervous. When they got to his room, he slid a tenspot to the desk clerk who nodded as they climbed the stairs to his room. Only two people were watching the blaring TV in the lobby.

"You give good head?" he asked as he unlocked the door to his room.

"Honey, I give the best head in this town." She walked into the room. He watched her take off her coat. He thought about her boyfriend and the cold hard pavement of the alley against his cut cheek. She had taken his money and laughed at him.

The whore looked a little scared. Good. He was glad. He could hear the noise of the TV from downstairs. He stared at her.

"Aren't you gonna take off those glasses?" she asked him, unbuttoning her dress.

He nodded. "In a minute. I wanna see what you look like naked with 'em on."

She laughed. "You look familiar. I thought I recognized you from some place —"

He took off his glasses.

Her voice caught in her throat as recognition spread across her face. Now she remembered him. But it was too late. She started to back up as he walked toward her.

"Now, wait a minute. Let's just talk a little. Your name's what? Gerry something? I know about you. I talked to some guys lookin' for you. I didn't tell 'em nothin'. So don't hurt me, okay?"

He didn't know how she knew his name and he didn't care. He had her backed into a corner and as she opened her mouth to scream, he smashed his fist into her mouth. Blood spurted from her nose and he clamped his hand down hard across her mouth. Throwing her across the bed, he ripped off her dress. She fought him. That made him mad.

He tore off part of the dress and stuffed it into her mouth. She choked, but he didn't care. Forcing her legs apart, he rolled her over onto her stomach. A wild, fierce joy surged through his body. He felt like singing. She writhed and he could feel the terror convulsing her body as she struggled to

157

breathe. To get away. He loved it. He was hard with joy as he pushed into her.

Her body screamed. No sound came from her mouth. But he could hear her body screaming. And no one else could hear.

Finally she was limp and he withdrew from her. He lay across her panting and then stood up. She wasn't moving. He turned her over roughly and saw her tongue, swollen and black, protruding from her mouth. The gag had come out. Her eyes were rolled back in her head. She was dead. He smiled and reached under the bed for the bat. As he raised the bat over his head he thought how mad he still was at her. Then he brought the bat down again and again on her dead body.

CHAPTER FOURTEEN

Michael watched out the front window as the police got into their car. Walking back into the kitchen, he looked at his cold TV dinner with disgust. He shuddered at the thought of eating and dumped the tray into the garbage can under the sink. Their questions had shaken him. He needed a stiff drink, not food.

He walked into the dining room and poured himself a small amount of Wild Turkey. Brian's face smiled at him from a photograph on his desk. He wished Brian were here. He needed him. Nothing rattled Brian. He would have handled the detectives' questions calmly.

Michael had just emerged from the shower when the doorbell rang; he had only had time to slip into a pair of sweatpants and pull a T-shirt over his head before answering the door. The police had let him go back and put on his shoes and socks before they told him about Trixie.

He took another swallow of Wild Turkey. He knew he had to call Caroline and Jane. He was putting it off. Mostly, he wanted to call Brian at his hotel in Lima but didn't know what time it was in Peru. And what would he tell Brian? That Trixie was dead and the police thought he and Brian knew who killed her? That would only upset him because there was nothing he could do.

Besides, Michael thought, the police had seemed satisfied with his answers. He thought they believed what he had told them. Jane and Caroline would back up his story and the whole mess would be straightened out.

Finally, Michael reached for the phone and dialed Jane's number. Caroline answered. Michael sat down on the leather ottoman beside the couch and put his glass on the rug beside him. "I think you better sit down."

"Is it Jane, Mike? Is something wrong with Jane?"

"No, no," he assured her. "Jane's at the gallery. She's fine. Uh — the police were here. They just left. You remember Trixie? The prostitute that Brian and I talked to?"

"Yes."

"She's dead. Murdered. They found her body in a

160

trash dumpster outside a boardinghouse on Ogden. They found a slip of paper in her purse that had my and Brian's name and phone number on it. So naturally, they showed up here to question us."

"Oh, my God," Caroline breathed.

"Yeah, well, it's under control now. I told them about Steckman and they found out he was staying in the boardinghouse. They think he dragged her body out onto the fire escape and threw her down into the dumpster . . . He strangled her, Caroline. He strangled her, raped her and then —"

"Stop, Michael. Where's Steckman now?"

"No one knows. The police have an all-points out on him."

"What's the address of the boardinghouse? Give it to me, Mike."

"It's not far from you guys, really." He gave her the address.

"Did you tell the police we were looking for Steckman? Did you tell them everything?"

"I told them he raped you and assaulted Evie and that you had asked us to help find him. That's all." He paused. "What else could I tell them? They'll find out eventually anyway. Besides, I want them to find him."

"Did you give them my name and address?"

"Yeah. They asked for it. They want to talk to you and Jane too."

"Okay. How long ago did they leave?"

"Just a few minutes ago. They seemed more interested in finding him than they did in talking to you. After all — he did kill somebody."

"That's right. Did you tell them where Jane was?"

"Yeah. Matty and Brooke's address too. I explained they were out of town. And I told them Brian was in Peru — that went over big. They thought we were dope smugglers too."

"Listen, Mike. I'm sorry about all this. Truly. I never should have dragged you and Brian in on this. I never should have dragged anyone in on it."

"Well, what are you going to do now?"

"I'm going down to the police station and tell them what happened. Tell them the truth and hope they've already caught him."

"Good idea," Michael said. "Don't even wait for them to come to you."

"I appreciate you calling me, Michael," Caroline said. "Really. I'm sorry about Trixie. And I'm sorry about you and Brian getting in trouble. But this just proves what I've been saying all along — he did kill somebody, finally."

"Are you going down to the gallery first — to tell Jane?"

"Would you mind going down there instead? Just tell her I went to talk to the police. Tell Jane not to worry. I can take care of myself."

"Huh?" Michael said, but Caroline had already hung up.

CHAPTER FIFTEEN

He almost didn't see the article until it was too late. He was sitting in a coffee shop with his sunglasses on and a dark baseball cap pulled down over his eyes. It was late evening. He was looking at the bus schedule trying to decide where to go because he knew he could no longer safely stay in Denver. He'd killed the whore.

He was drinking his coffee and trying to decide how far he could go on the whore's money when he saw the newspaper on the seat beside him. A small weekly paper, not the *Post* or *News,* and he almost didn't pick it up. But something on the front page of the paper caught his eyes.

Right on the front page was the car. That fancy Thunderbird he'd seen the Jordan woman driving the night she almost ran over him. The car was parked in front of a big house. He slowly read the article. It was about some woman artist who was opening a gallery. He read the article carefully. It was all about women and their businesses.

He looked at the car closely, at the hood ornament. He knew it was the same car. The article gave the address of the house in the picture. It wasn't far from where he was. And it wasn't far from where he had seen the car the night he had the nurse. He read the article again. There was no mention of Caroline Jordan in the article. Only the woman artist. So they lived together. They were probably dykes or some shit. He smiled. He had ruined her for other men. He laughed aloud.

He finished his cup of coffee, picked up his duffel bag and started walking. He knew she'd be glad to see him.

CHAPTER SIXTEEN

For a long time after Michael's call, Caroline stared out the window into the darkness. She felt drained and overwhelmingly disappointed. Steckman was gone. The room where he had stayed for months, only blocks from where she lived, would be empty when she got there. And the police would be everywhere. She would have to be careful. They might have gotten a description of her from Michael. There wasn't much time. Michael would give Jane her message and Caroline knew Jane would try to stop her. And then there were the police. They had found Michael. They would find her too.

She went into her bedroom and changed into dark jeans, a black T-shirt and a windbreaker. It was warm for the windbreaker but she needed something to conceal the gun. She removed the revolver from the corner of her dresser drawer and, after checking the safety and making sure the cylinder was full and that she had extra bullets in her windbreaker pocket, she slipped the .38 into the waistband of her jeans. In the hall closet, she found an old baseball cap which she put on, tucking up her hair. After checking her appearance in the hallway mirror, Caroline walked to the kitchen and turned off the light. There was lightning over the mountains and she heard a distant clap of thunder. A gust of wind rustled the leaves on the bushes next to the house. Another thunderstorm.

She turned away from the window and stood in the darkness. The familiar outlines of the kitchen chairs around the table, the comforting bulk of the refrigerator, the muted bars of light that patterned the linoleum, all reassured her with their ordinary presence. She checked the lock on the back door and in a flash of lightning from the thunderstorm that was now over the city, she saw movement in the backyard.

Someone was coming over the fence.

"What?" Jane put down the paint roller and stared at Michael in disbelief. "And you gave it to her — just like that?"

166

Michael spread his hands. "What's the difference, Jane? She said she was going downtown to talk to the cops right after we hung up. She said not to worry — she could take care of herself."

"What do you think *that* means? Why would she say that if she was just going downtown to talk to the cops? You shouldn't have told her the address." Jane wiped her hands on a rag.

"I don't see what you're getting so upset about. He's not there anyway. Even Caroline knows that. He's long gone."

"She has a gun, Michael. For weeks she's been practicing with it and walking around at night looking for him."

"That's ridiculous."

"Tell her that. She thinks it's her last chance to get him. Now I admit, she won't see him. But what if she *thinks* she sees him and takes a potshot at somebody?"

"Well, what do you want to do about it? Shall we go down to the address and see if she's there?"

Jane thought a moment. "No, I think I should go home and see if she's still there. You call the cops and tell them what happened. If she's not at home, then I'll call you."

Outside, the storm raged. "God, look at the rain. I better get going. I have this feeling —" She grabbed the keys to her Jeep and rushed to the door.

He saw the light go off in the kitchen just as he was jumping the fence. A shadow of someone moved around inside the house. He hid by the fence and surveyed the backyard. A sudden flash of lightning illuminated a large rose garden, lawn furniture on a patio close to the house, and a small unattached garage. He edged along the fence, staying in the shadows until he reached the garage. The Thunderbird was parked in the gravel driveway. Rain started to pelt his face and a deafening clap of thunder exploded overhead. He smiled and turned toward the house.

Caroline knew who was coming over the fence. She watched him stop by the fence and then creep toward the garage. Her heart was pounding; every nerve in her body throbbed. She held her hands up to her face in the dim light of the kitchen and saw that they were shaking.

Somehow the trembling provided her with the physical impetus she needed. She walked quickly down the hallway to the foyer. She switched off the front porch light. Then she walked over to the stairway and sat down in the darkness on the fourth step next to the light switch. Rain lashed at the windows, and the wind whipped through the trees. Thunder shook the house with unbelievable force. She took the gun from her waistband and released the safety. Power flowed from the gun into her body. Her mind, which had been clogged with fear, began to function again. She was in control.

Of all the possible outcomes she could have imagined, this was the best. Everything had suddenly turned to her advantage. Steckman thought *he* was the hunter. But he was wrong. The prey was lying in wait. It would be simple. A simple case of self-defense. She remembered him clearly, his face distorted with rage as he screamed at her: "I'll get you, you lying whore. I'll get you. I'll find you."

Her hand tightened on the gun when she heard the glass break in the kitchen, a fumbling sound as he reached inside and the lock on the kitchen door clicked. The door squeaked on its hinges as it opened slowly. He was in the house. She could hear his breathing.

The house was too quiet. She might have gone to bed. But it was still too quiet. He didn't like the way the house felt. He pawed the wall and felt the telephone cord. He unplugged it. Something felt wrong to him.

He felt his way down the hallway, his eyes adjusting to the dark. He was beginning to see more clearly. At the end of the hallway, he stopped. Too late. He heard a small movement, a little noise to his right. Then the lights were on and he was blinded. He threw himself against the wall and looked up.

"Hello, Gerry." Caroline held the gun with steady hands. Her voice was calm. "Glad you found your way in. I was hoping you wouldn't ring the doorbell. I wanted you to break in. That way I can kill you and get away with it."

Caroline looked at Gerald Steckman closely. He looked different. The last time she had seen him, he had been choked with rage. The verdict had only fueled his anger. Now he looked older, even frail. His skin was pasty except for the angry red scar still visible through his scraggly beard. He looked trapped, Caroline thought triumphantly.

His eyes darted around the foyer, and he pressed his hands against the wall to steady himself. "You don't know how to use that." He pointed to the gun. "Even if you did know how, you wouldn't."

Caroline felt a surge of joy sweep through her. She moved the gun slightly and fired a quick shot six inches from his head. She watched with satisfaction as a wet stain spread across the front of his pants. The bullet had blasted bits of plaster from the wall onto his shoulder and these fell as he slid down the wall to a sitting position.

"Good, you stay there." Caroline kept the gun on him. "I'm going to kill you, Gerry. You tried to ruin my life." She moved down a step closer to him. Her throat strained, as if she were instructing her class on a particularly difficult point. "You tried to rape my friend's little girl. You hurt her. I want you to understand why I'm going to kill you. I don't care that you're not sorry. I know you're not. I don't want you to beg forgiveness anyway. I just want you to listen. Will you do that?"

Steckman did not answer, but his eyes betrayed his fear and impotence. He did not take his eyes off the gun.

Caroline smiled. She had his attention.

She was talking to him but he wasn't listening. He watched her mouth move around the words. He remembered when she had testified at his trial. Years ago. She wore a blue dress and big silver earrings. He could tell then she was still frightened. When she looked at him then from behind the lawyers, she was afraid. He had liked that.

She didn't look scared now. He watched the gun.

"I think the reason you rape women is because you like to have power over them. It makes you feel strong."

"Yeah, bitch. I heard that before from the shrinks. You don't know shit."

"I know how you feel now," Caroline went on as though he hadn't spoken. "I know because I feel that way too. I feel strong. I know you can't hurt me. I'm not going to feel sorry after I kill you either."

A fierce gust of wind rattled the windows and lightning ripped across the sky. Thunder followed lightning almost immediately and lightning flashed again.

"I don't even know why I'm talking to you like a normal person." Caroline shook her head. "You're a monster. You don't understand. I might as well kill you now." She pointed the gun at him. Her hand was steady.

"Don't shoot me," he pleaded suddenly. "Please don't kill me." He began to cry and Caroline hesitated. His cries were nearly extinguished by the fierce, continuous thunder and lightning of the storm. Suddenly, a roll of thunder followed by a horrible cracking sound split the air. It sounded as if a tree had been split down the middle.

171

The light in the hallway flickered once.
Then it was dark.

Jane sat at the stoplight tapping her foot on the accelerator impatiently. "Come on, come on," she muttered. Then she ran the red light. The streets were slick with rain and huge broken limbs were scattered in the street and across the lawns. The wind had stripped leaves from the trees; they blanketed the streets and sidewalks. As the lightning and thunder raged overhead, Jane remembered how terrified Caroline was of thunderstorms. She hoped she wasn't home alone feeling frightened.

"I'm coming, honey," she said as she swerved to avoid a huge limb lying in the street. "I'm coming."

Caroline sat in the blackness for a moment before she realized Steckman was no longer in front of her. The next instant, she realized she didn't know where he was, and she scrambled up the stairs to the landing. She crouched against the wall and listened.

In a lull between thunder and lightning, she thought she heard a noise in the front room. The fear which she had successfully controlled when she had first seen him climb over the fence in the backyard washed over her again.

She crawled on her hands and knees up the remaining stairs and hurried down the hall to Jane's studio. Her easel was a spindly outline against the unshaded window. For an instant, the easel's familiar shape comforted her, calmed her fear. Then another crash of thunder exploded, and Caroline scuttled behind an overstuffed chair in the corner of the studio and wedged herself between the chair and the wall.

With the gun still clenched in her hand and darkness surrounding her, she tried to evoke some thought or image that would help her regain control of the terrible fear that now ruled her.

Nothing came to mind.

Crammed behind the chair, she suddenly remembered watching Flash Gordon as a child. Who was the villain in Flash Gordon? She tried to remember.

"Ming the Merciless," Caroline whispered. She stifled a hysterical giggle. She remembered huddling behind the couch with her official Flash Gordon Space Blaster — acquired with two Cheerios boxtops and fifty cents — and listening to the unbearably scary drama from the unseen television set.

"Why do you stay in here if you're so scared?" her father had asked her. "Turn off the TV and go play with your dollies if you're that scared."

"No. Don't turn it off. I like to be scared. It helps me not be scared later," Caroline had answered, gripping her Space Blaster even tighter.

Now she gripped the pistol tighter and strained to hear any movements Steckman might be making. The storm had finally passed over and she could hear better.

For a long time, she heard nothing. Only the sound of water dripping from the eaves of the house and a rustle of fallen leaves in the gutters. She wanted to go to the light switch to see if the electricity was on. But the same inertia that kept her hidden behind the couch during Flash Gordon when she was a child now riveted her to the floor behind the chair. All of the competence and power the gun had instilled in her was gone. She felt as helpless and frightened as she had as a child.

A sound from below made her close her eyes. Her body became even more rigid with fear.

He was opening drawers in the kitchen.

The woman had run from him again, her movements quick and frantic. She was afraid of him again. He could smell her fear. Just for a second, he thought, he had almost lost his nerve. His taste for the hunt. Then the lights went out and she ran.

He went into the kitchen. It didn't matter now that she had a gun. She wouldn't use it.

He opened the drawers in the kitchen until he found a knife. He tested the edge on the pad of his thumb. It was sharp enough to make the whore upstairs sorry she had sent him to prison. He would make her sorry that she had shot at his head and made him wet his pants.

He would cut her head off.

Jane pulled into the driveway of her house in total darkness. She had never realized how much light came from streetlights. She sat in the driveway with her headlights on, suddenly uneasy, wary of what the night was hiding. No lights were on in the house but Caroline's car was in the driveway. A good sign, Jane thought. If she had already left, surely she would have taken the car.

Having armed herself with this face, Jane opened the door of her Jeep and began walking toward the front door.

Caroline heard the Jeep pull in. Still immobilized by fear, she imagined Jane coming up the steps of the house and inserting her key in the lock. She imagined Steckman creeping through the house, in the dark, hiding behind the front door. He had a knife in his hand and when Jane opened the door, he would slit her throat.

Caroline jerked upright, as if yanked violently by invisible strings. The gun gripped tightly in her sweating hand, she stumbled to the top of the stairway. When she reached the landing, she looked around the corner and saw Jane's vague form through the window in the front door as she fumbled in the dark with her keys.

She turned and saw Steckman's form pressed against the wall behind the door. A knife blade glinted.

Jane turned her key in the lock and pushed the heavy oak door open. The same uneasy feeling of dread that had overwhelmed her in the driveway gripped her again. She paused. Forgetting that the lights were out, she reached up to pull the chain hanging from the light fixture.

Something from behind the door smashed into her arm, and she felt a searing pain run from her wrist to the top of her shoulder. She stumbled into the hallway and fell forward on her face. Stunned, she felt warm, sticky liquid that she knew dimly must be blood running down her arm. She tried to pull herself upright — she knew she had to get up and get away before —

She couldn't move. Someone was yelling her name, an unearthly screaming. The sound came from the stairway. Caroline? She turned her head, but the pool of blood on the floor was widening and she was losing consciousness. She looked at the blood and saw a pair of legs. Some part of her knew the legs belonged to the person behind the door who had stabbed her. But she couldn't get away. She was too weak.

Then an explosion. Had the storm returned? The legs crumpled, and she felt the floor shake as a body fell beside her.

Lights suddenly blinded her, and she rested her face on the floor. Staring at her, were the dead open eyes of Gerald Steckman.

CHAPTER SEVENTEEN

"Are you sure you want to do this?" Caroline asked Jane. They were sitting in Caroline's Thunderbird outside the Steel Magnolia. Jane shifted her heavily bandaged arm inside the sling and continued to stare out the window. "Jane?"

"No, I'm not sure. But we haven't seen them since they got back from their vacation. They're anxious to hear it from us in person. Brooke'll want all the gory details. You know how she is." She turned to Caroline with an accusing stare. "Besides, I'm sure they want to see you before you leave."

Caroline looked at her with exasperation. "Oh, for God's sake!"

"Well, how do you expect me to feel? Am I supposed to be dancing in the streets because you're going to leave me?" She shook her head. "You *promised.* You promised if I moved here, you'd never leave me again."

"I know I promised. I expected you to be upset. I understand and I'm sorry. But I also expect you to understand why I have to get away. And I'm not leaving you again. It's not like the first time. I'm coming back."

"I think nine months is a long time."

"That's just how long my leave of absence is from work," Caroline said. "I'll probably come back sooner."

"Ha! Anything could happen."

Caroline nodded. "Yeah, you could take up with Gretel Weisman while I'm gone. Someone who's not so crazy."

"I don't want somebody else," Jane said fiercely. "I want you."

"You have me," Caroline said with equal fervor. "Believe me, I'll never let you go. You know too much." She put her hand on Jane's arm. "Come on, sweetie. Let's go."

They walked to the front door of the Steel Magnolia and stood there for a moment. "You know I love you, don't you Janie?" Caroline whispered. "I'm not leaving until after the gallery opens."

"I know." She looked at her lover. "You saved my life. I guess that means something."

Caroline grinned. "You better believe it."

178

They walked into the bar. As usual it was jammed with women sitting at tables, standing around the pool tables and crowding the bar. Jane saw Margaret behind the bar and waved. Margaret reached under the bar and flipped the jukebox off. As they stood in the doorway, the bar gradually grew quiet as women stopped playing pool, dancing and talking.

Jane saw Matty and Brooke sitting at a table near the bar. They stood up. Suddenly, all around them, women rose to their feet until everyone in the bar was standing. Jane saw Sandy come out of the kitchen, drying her hands on her apron.

Then everyone began to applaud.

Jane grinned as Brooke walked toward her cheering and raising a clenched fist. She grabbed Jane and hugged her ferociously.

"Hey, watch the arm," Jane cautioned.

"Holy shit, you're wounded," Brooke shouted. "Hey, Margaret! Drinks for these warriors. Let's have a toast everybody."

Women cheered and raised their glasses. Jane looked at Caroline who was standing with her arms around Matty. They were both crying. After everyone in the bar toasted the heroes, they sat down at the table.

"Well, we were planning on boring the shit out of you when we got back with home movies of Disneyworld and New Orleans, but I guess more exciting things are going to take precedent." Brooke pressed Jane's left arm. "Tell us all. Details. Give us details."

"We told you everything on the phone," Caroline insisted.

"I know. But we've been wondering," Matty interjected. "How did he know where you lived?"

Jane looked guilty. "It was that damn interview with Gretel in the *Cherry Creek News*. The police found it in his pocket. He saw Caroline's car in the picture and the address was right there. Stupid."

"How's the arm?" Brooke asked softly, putting her arm gently around Jane.

"Better," Jane said gruffly. "It'll be okay. We're going ahead with the opening. The invitations were already printed up and I'm ready — pretty much."

"Yeah," Caroline said teasingly. "We don't want to disappoint Gretel. I can't wait to see this woman."

"Did they have to give you a transfusion?" Brooke asked.

"Yeah."

"How many stitches?"

"God, Brooke. Do you always need the gruesome details?" Matty chided her.

"I like gruesome details. How many?"

"One-hundred-and-thirty-two." Jane shifted her arm a little.

"Holy shit!" Brooke exclaimed. "Is it going to be okay? That's your drawing arm, for God's sake."

"Yeah, they think it'll be okay. He cut some tendons, but they sewed them back together. I've got some physical therapy coming up after the stitches come out. I'm pretty lucky. Thanks to Carrie."

"Yeah." Brooke laughed. "How about that? Ol' Dead-eye. Where'd you learn to shoot like that?"

"Lots of practice," Caroline said briefly.

"It's amazing. You could easily have missed and shot Janie instead," Matty said with admiration. "That was incredible shooting."

"Hey, what's all this shit about you going away?" Brooke asked.

Caroline looked at Jane. "I'm just taking some time off. That's all."

"Like a vacation?" Matty asked. "A couple weeks?"

"No, a little longer than that. I got a leave of absence from school. I'll be gone about nine months."

"Where are you going?" Brooke asked.

"I'm going to Illinois first," Caroline told them. "I have relatives in Charleston. I'll probably visit them. Then I may go East. I don't know. I need some time to sort things out."

"Why are you leaving?" Brooke asked bluntly.

"That's what Janie keeps asking me."

"Do you think you're running away?" Matty asked softly.

"No, absolutely not," Caroline said vehemently. "I've spent most of my adult life running away. I never came to terms with the rape — I ran away to California and met Jane. And then when that got to be too much for me, I ran away from her. I think I need to stop and figure it out." She smiled warmly at her friends. "Believe me, you're not getting rid of me permanently. I'll be back."

"Are you going to sell the house?" Brooke asked.

"God, no. I'm not leaving for good, Brooke. I told you that. And I'm counting on you to keep an eye on the famous artist here while I'm gone. Now that the gallery is opening, women will be hanging all over her. I don't want to come back here and find that Gretel What's-Her-Name installed in my house."

Even Jane laughed.

"Well, we'll miss you while you're gone," Matty

said. "But we'll be here when you get back." She raised her glass. "Let's have a toast."

They raised their glasses.

"To us," Matty said.

"To friendship," Brooke added.

"To love," Jane said, looking at Caroline.

"May it never end," Caroline finished.

A few of the publications of
THE NAIAD PRESS, INC.
P.O. Box 10543 • Tallahassee, Florida 32302
Phone (904) 539-5965
Mail orders welcome. Please include 15% postage.

CALLING RAIN by Karen Marie Christa Minns. 240 pp.
Spellbinding, erotic love story ISBN 0-941483-87-8 $9.95

BLACK IRIS by Jeane Harris. 192 pp. Caroline's hidden past . . .
ISBN 0-941483-68-1 8.95

TOUCHWOOD by Karin Kallmaker. 240 pp. Loving, May/
December romance. ISBN 0-941483-76-2 8.95

BAYOU CITY SECRETS by Deborah Powell. 224 pp. A Hollis
Carpenter mystery. First in a series. ISBN 0-941483-91-6 8.95

COP OUT by Claire McNab. 208 pp. 4th Det. Insp. Carol Ashton
mystery. ISBN 0-941483-84-3 8.95

LODESTAR by Phyllis Horn. 224 pp. Romantic, fast-moving
adventure. ISBN 0-941483-83-5 8.95

THE BEVERLY MALIBU by Katherine V. Forrest. 288 pp. A
Kate Delafield Mystery. 3rd in a series. (HC) ISBN 0-941483-47-9 16.95
Paperback ISBN 0-941483-48-7 9.95

THAT OLD STUDEBAKER by Lee Lynch. 272 pp. Andy's affair
with Regina and her attachment to her beloved car.
ISBN 0-941483-82-7 9.95

PASSION'S LEGACY by Lori Paige. 224 pp. Sarah is swept into
the arms of Augusta Pym in this delightful historical romance.
ISBN 0-941483-81-9 8.95

THE PROVIDENCE FILE by Amanda Kyle Williams. 256 pp.
Second espionage thriller featuring lesbian agent Madison McGuire
ISBN 0-941483-92-4 8.95

I LEFT MY HEART by Jaye Maiman. 320 pp. A Robin Miller
Mystery. First in a series. ISBN 0-941483-72-X 9.95

THE PRICE OF SALT by Patricia Highsmith (writing as Claire
Morgan). 288 pp. Classic lesbian novel, first issued in 1952 . . .
acknowledged by its author under her own, very famous, name.
ISBN 1-56280-003-5 8.95

SIDE BY SIDE by Isabel Miller. 256 pp. From beloved author of
Patience and Sarah. ISBN 0-941483-77-0 8.95

SOUTHBOUND by Sheila Ortiz Taylor. 240 pp. Hilarious sequel
to *Faultline.* ISBN 0-941483-78-9 8.95

STAYING POWER: LONG TERM LESBIAN COUPLES
by Susan E. Johnson. 352 pp. Joys of coupledom.
ISBN 0-941-483-75-4   12.95

SLICK by Camarin Grae. 304 pp. Exotic, erotic adventure.
ISBN 0-941483-74-6   9.95

NINTH LIFE by Lauren Wright Douglas. 256 pp. A Caitlin
Reece mystery. 2nd in a series.   ISBN 0-941483-50-9   8.95

PLAYERS by Robbi Sommers. 192 pp. Sizzling, erotic novel.
ISBN 0-941483-73-8   8.95

MURDER AT RED ROOK RANCH by Dorothy Tell. 224 pp.
First Poppy Dillworth adventure.   ISBN 0-941483-80-0   8.95

LESBIAN SURVIVAL MANUAL by Rhonda Dicksion.
112 pp. Cartoons!   ISBN 0-941483-71-1   8.95

A ROOM FULL OF WOMEN by Elisabeth Nonas. 256 pp.
Contemporary Lesbian lives.   ISBN 0-941483-69-X   8.95

MURDER IS RELATIVE by Karen Saum. 256 pp. The first
Brigid Donovan mystery.   ISBN 0-941483-70-3   8.95

PRIORITIES by Lynda Lyons 288 pp. Science fiction with
a twist.   ISBN 0-941483-66-5   8.95

THEME FOR DIVERSE INSTRUMENTS by Jane Rule. 208
pp. Powerful romantic lesbian stories.   ISBN 0-941483-63-0   8.95

LESBIAN QUERIES by Hertz & Ertman. 112 pp. The questions
you were too embarrassed to ask.   ISBN 0-941483-67-3   8.95

CLUB 12 by Amanda Kyle Williams. 288 pp. Espionage thriller
featuring a lesbian agent!   ISBN 0-941483-64-9   8.95

DEATH DOWN UNDER by Claire McNab. 240 pp. 3rd Det.
Insp. Carol Ashton mystery.   ISBN 0-941483-39-8   8.95

MONTANA FEATHERS by Penny Hayes. 256 pp. Vivian and
Elizabeth find love in frontier Montana.   ISBN 0-941483-61-4   8.95

CHESAPEAKE PROJECT by Phyllis Horn. 304 pp. Jessie &
Meredith in perilous adventure.   ISBN 0-941483-58-4   8.95

LIFESTYLES by Jackie Calhoun. 224 pp. Contemporary Lesbian
lives and loves.   ISBN 0-941483-57-6   8.95

VIRAGO by Karen Marie Christa Minns. 208 pp. Darsen has
chosen Ginny.   ISBN 0-941483-56-8   8.95

WILDERNESS TREK by Dorothy Tell. 192 pp. Six women on
vacation learning "new" skills.   ISBN 0-941483-60-6   8.95

MURDER BY THE BOOK by Pat Welch. 256 pp. A Helen
Black Mystery. First in a series.   ISBN 0-941483-59-2   8.95

BERRIGAN by Vicki P. McConnell. 176 pp. Youthful Lesbian —
romantic, idealistic Berrigan.   ISBN 0-941483-55-X   8.95

LESBIANS IN GERMANY by Lillian Faderman & B. Eriksson.
128 pp. Fiction, poetry, essays.   ISBN 0-941483-62-2   8.95

THERE'S SOMETHING I'VE BEEN MEANING TO TELL
YOU Ed. by Loralee MacPike. 288 pp. Gay men and lesbians
coming out to their children.   ISBN 0-941483-44-4   9.95
                                        ISBN 0-941483-54-1   16.95

LIFTING BELLY by Gertrude Stein. Ed. by Rebecca Mark. 104
pp. Erotic poetry.   ISBN 0-941483-51-7   8.95
                                        ISBN 0-941483-53-3   14.95

ROSE PENSKI by Roz Perry. 192 pp. Adult lovers in a long-term
relationship.   ISBN 0-941483-37-1   8.95

AFTER THE FIRE by Jane Rule. 256 pp. Warm, human novel
by this incomparable author.   ISBN 0-941483-45-2   8.95

SUE SLATE, PRIVATE EYE by Lee Lynch. 176 pp. The gay
folk of Peacock Alley are *all cats*. ISBN 0-941483-52-5   8.95

CHRIS by Randy Salem. 224 pp. Golden oldie. Handsome Chris
and her adventures.   ISBN 0-941483-42-8   8.95

THREE WOMEN by March Hastings. 232 pp. Golden oldie. A
triangle among wealthy sophisticates. ISBN 0-941483-43-6   8.95

RICE AND BEANS by Valeria Taylor. 232 pp. Love and
romance on poverty row.   ISBN 0-941483-41-X   8.95

PLEASURES by Robbi Sommers. 204 pp. Unprecedented
eroticism.   ISBN 0-941483-49-5   8.95

EDGEWISE by Camarin Grae. 372 pp. Spellbinding
adventure.   ISBN 0-941483-19-3   9.95

FATAL REUNION by Claire McNab. 224 pp. 2nd Det. Inspec.
Carol Ashton mystery.   ISBN 0-941483-40-1   8.95

KEEP TO ME STRANGER by Sarah Aldridge. 372 pp. Romance
set in a department store dynasty.   ISBN 0-941483-38-X   9.95

HEARTSCAPE by Sue Gambill. 204 pp. American lesbian in
Portugal.   ISBN 0-941483-33-9   8.95

IN THE BLOOD by Lauren Wright Douglas. 252 pp. Lesbian
science fiction adventure fantasy   ISBN 0-941483-22-3   8.95

THE BEE'S KISS by Shirley Verel. 216 pp. Delicate, delicious
romance.   ISBN 0-941483-36-3   8.95

RAGING MOTHER MOUNTAIN by Pat Emmerson. 264 pp.
Furosa Firechild's adventures in Wonderland.   ISBN 0-941483-35-5   8.95

IN EVERY PORT by Karin Kallmaker. 228 pp. Jessica's sexy,
adventuresome travels.   ISBN 0-941483-37-7   8.95

OF LOVE AND GLORY by Evelyn Kennedy. 192 pp. Exciting
WWII romance.   ISBN 0-941483-32-0   8.95

CLICKING STONES by Nancy Tyler Glenn. 288 pp. Love
transcending time.   ISBN 0-941483-31-2   8.95

SURVIVING SISTERS by Gail Pass. 252 pp. Powerful love
story.   ISBN 0-941483-16-9   8.95

SOUTH OF THE LINE by Catherine Ennis. 216 pp. Civil War
adventure.   ISBN 0-941483-29-0   8.95

WOMAN PLUS WOMAN by Dolores Klaich. 300 pp. Supurb
Lesbian overview.   ISBN 0-941483-28-2   9.95

SLOW DANCING AT MISS POLLY'S by Sheila Ortiz Taylor.
96 pp. Lesbian Poetry   ISBN 0-941483-30-4   7.95

DOUBLE DAUGHTER by Vicki P. McConnell. 216 pp. A Nyla
Wade Mystery, third in the series.   ISBN 0-941483-26-6   8.95

HEAVY GILT by Delores Klaich. 192 pp. Lesbian detective/
disappearing homophobes/upper class gay society.

                                            ISBN 0-941483-25-8   8.95

THE FINER GRAIN by Denise Ohio. 216 pp. Brilliant young
college lesbian novel.   ISBN 0-941483-11-8   8.95

THE AMAZON TRAIL by Lee Lynch. 216 pp. Life, travel & lore
of famous lesbian author.   ISBN 0-941483-27-4   8.95

HIGH CONTRAST by Jessie Lattimore. 264 pp. Women of the
Crystal Palace.   ISBN 0-941483-17-7   8.95

OCTOBER OBSESSION by Meredith More. Josie's rich, secret
Lesbian life.   ISBN 0-941483-18-5   8.95

LESBIAN CROSSROADS by Ruth Baetz. 276 pp. Contemporary
Lesbian lives.   ISBN 0-941483-21-5   9.95

BEFORE STONEWALL: THE MAKING OF A GAY AND
LESBIAN COMMUNITY by Andrea Weiss & Greta Schiller.
96 pp., 25 illus.   ISBN 0-941483-20-7   7.95

WE WALK THE BACK OF THE TIGER by Patricia A. Murphy.
192 pp. Romantic Lesbian novel/beginning women's movement.
                                            ISBN 0-941483-13-4   8.95

SUNDAY'S CHILD by Joyce Bright. 216 pp. Lesbian athletics, at
last the novel about sports.   ISBN 0-941483-12-6   8.95

OSTEN'S BAY by Zenobia N. Vole. 204 pp. Sizzling adventure
romance set on Bonaire.   ISBN 0-941483-15-0   8.95

These are just a few of the many Naiad Press titles — we are the oldest and
largest lesbian/feminist publishing company in the world. Please request a
complete catalog. We offer personal service; we encourage and welcome direct
mail orders from individuals who have limited access to bookstores carrying
our publications.